THE

Other
Woman

Also by Rona Jaffe

THE
Other
Woman

RONA JAFFE

wm

WILLIAM MORROW
An Imprint of HarperCollins*Publishers*

A hardcover edition of this book was published by William Morrow in 1972.

The first paperback edition was published in 1980 by Dell.

This book is a work of fiction. The characters, incidents, and dialogue are drawn from the author's imagination and are not to be construed as real. Any resemblance to actual events or persons, living or dead, is entirely coincidental.

HarperCollins books may be purchased for educational, business, or sales promotional use. For information please e-mail the Special Markets Department at SPsales@harpercollins.com.

FIRST WILLIAM MORROW PAPERBACK EDITION PUBLISHED 2014.

Library of Congress Cataloging-in-Publication Data has been applied for.

ISBN 978-0-06-239723-2

14 15 16 17 18   OV/RRD   10 9 8 7 6 5 4 3 2 1

THE

Other
Woman

1

When Carol Prince was fourteen she wrote in her diary: "Someday I am going to be important." She did become important, but in a way she least expected.

She hated her childhood, a prison filled with words like "obedience" and "respect," and she had hardly been able to wait to serve her term. Twenty-one was perfect, the day she knew her parents could no longer threaten to send her to a home for wayward girls if she broke their rules. Having recently lost twenty pounds—the prison in which she had protected her virginity—she celebrated her twenty-first birthday by dragging an older man who was in love with her to a sleazy hotel and losing her virginity at last. Then she went home to her parents' clean East Side apartment, with the indestructible silk flowers and the pinned-on arm covers on all the chairs, and allowed them to treat her to a birthday dinner at Longchamps complete with a domestic champagne cocktail. Her mother had suggested she not bring a date. She had not intended to: the young men she knew would take Dinner With The Family as too much encouragement for their plans of making her the perfect wife of a rising young accountant or medical student and the mother of his children. She did not intend to be anyone's wife or mother, she intended to be a journalist and travel the world. This was all in 1953, when virginity was important, homes for wayward girls were not in the newspapers but in the imagination of puritanical middle-class mothers and their frightened daughters, and mothers who bought silk flowers instead of plastic ones were considered to have taste.

Carol and her mother bought their clothes in the same stores and had their hair done in the same salon, which was on Madison Avenue and was called a Beauty Parlor. Carol had a permanent. She always wore black in the evening. Her mother paid for her clothes and therefore felt free to choose them. Her mother had also bought her four actual girdles, with zippers up the side, and when Carol became fashionably skinny she put the girdles into the kitchen sink one day when the maid was off and her mother was at a charity luncheon and burned them. They made a strange smell. Then she took a pair of scissors and cut off her permanent (it was frizzy anyway) and thus became the first girl in New York to have what would later be known as the Sassoon Cut. That night her mother cried. She had three curls of Carol's reddish baby hair tied with a bow and wrapped in tissue paper in her bottom bureau drawer, the bureau with the fat cupids painted on the front, and now her daughter's hair had not only turned dark but it looked as if "rats had nibbled at it."

The reason Carol let her mother buy her clothes was simple: she was saving all the money from her dreary job in a small publishing company for her escape. Being of legal majority, she now rented an apartment in a rent-controlled building with free venetian blinds. Her mother cried again. Her aunt, who was more modern than her mother, told her to buy a queen-size bed because it was more comfortable. Carol did, becoming the only one of her unmarried friends who owned such a thing. The rest of them made do on the single beds they had brought from home. It was considered more feminine to sleep at the man's house. She still remembered the sleazy hotel with affection, although the carpet had smelled faintly of urine and you had to put money into the radio to make it play. She remembered the physical affair with affection too, if not with passion, since the only thing interesting about it was that she had done it. The man remained her friend. He had a wife, and he felt free to love Carol as much as he wanted to since she did not love him back. She had a crush on him, though, since he was a journalist, what she wanted to be. He taught her how to write an article, what a lead was, how to build suspense. Occasionally he let her be his chauffeur when he went to interview people out of town. Once he interviewed a gangster: the house was bugged and they had to talk on the lawn. The wind was blowing furiously and the gangster looked like a gray-haired businessman. Later they discovered that someone had ripped the interior of the journalist's car apart, looking for who knows what. Carol found this very glamorous.

She had always had a great appeal for older men.

They found her amusing because she always wanted to know things. She was a hard worker, she laughed a lot, she could drink as much as they could, and she looked so vulnerable to them in her black dresses that were too old for her, with her chopped-off hair and big eyes like searchlights. She was never abashed to stare at people in elevators and on the street. Everything in life was to be stored and used. She always had an older man in her life, and a young one. The young one was for the world, the older one was for herself. At that time being involved with an older man (older men were inevitably married) was considered a sickness. It meant you wanted the unattainable. To Carol it meant information. She could not imagine spending time with someone you could not learn from. There was so much to learn, and she knew so little. She used her experience with older men to write her first published article in a major magazine: "Girls Who Look for Father Figures." She felt it was a complete lie, but it was the only approach the magazine would accept, and she wanted to see her name in print as quickly as possible.

She became rather an expert on maladies of the mind and heart, provided she was careful to point out that anything that deviated from the norm—marriage, home, babies—led to unhappiness. By the time she was twenty-six she was making a lot of money for a girl her age, and she had quit her job to write full time. Her boss offered to say he had fired her so she could collect unemployment; after all, she had worked six years and it would be a handy sum. She was too proud to accept his offer. "This is the only office job I will ever have," she told him, "and I don't want to say I was fired."

There were times afterward she regretted not having the unemployment money, but she did not regret it very much. It eroded her pride to have to write articles she did not believe in, and knowing she was independent helped make up for it. She thought up more interesting ideas for articles, interviews with celebrities, and began to travel. All her friends from high school had married and she had been a bridesmaid several times. Her college friends had married too, but she did not see them anymore because the ones she liked did not live in New York. She now had her name on magazine covers occasionally, and she had a certain following and received fan letters, some of them from men proposing marriage. She wrote a piece on lonely people who wrote love letters to strangers. It was the first piece she had written with heart, and afterward she had to have her telephone number unlisted.

Her mother and her mother's friends viewed her rising career with dismay. Her mother said, "Boys don't want to marry girls who are too independent."

Because everyone she met at parties talked about their analysis, Carol treated herself to a year of analysis to find out why she had never married. The doctor asked her immediately if she wanted a penis. She had never thought about it. She thought about it there in his office. "No," she said finally. "If I did, it might be small, and then I would feel badly about that. That sort of thing seems to be a big concern to men." The doctor looked embarrassed. She wondered if he had a small one. He was just a man to her, she couldn't think of him as a doctor or an authority, although once when she had a sore throat she asked him to look at it since she was paying him anyway, and he prescribed some pills. She was aware that he thought she was funny and interesting because he laughed a lot at the things she said. She also became aware after a few months that he didn't think she was sick, or at least what he considered her sickness was that she did not fit into the role he saw for her as a young woman.

"You are lonely," he said. "I would like to see you married. You would be a wonderful mother."

"But I really don't feel I'm ready for that. There are so many things I haven't done yet."

"You're lucky you can write. You can stay at home with the children and write."

"Only if they're zombies," she said.

"You could marry a rich man. You could have a nurse for the children."

"Then why have them? If I had kids I'd want to enjoy being with them."

"Your parents must have made you feel very unwanted," he said sadly.

"Unwanted? They never let me out of their sight."

"You must understand you are rejecting being feminine."

"If being feminine means washing some guy's socks, then how come every Chinese laundryman down on the corner doesn't feel his masculinity threatened?"

"You retreat into words," he said.

"That's how I express myself."

"You could express yourself as a woman if you had a man to take care of you."

"Then how come I don't fall in love?" Carol asked. "I *think* I'm in love, but I know I'm really not. I just like them. Sometimes I don't even like them very much. I just like some things about them. Or I like that they're there. I'd get married if I could find somebody I really loved."

"There have been cases where love came afterward."

"You mean a marriage of convenience?" she said, horrified.

"It has worked."

Not for me, she thought. "Do you think I'm really neurotic?" she asked.

"The only area in which you function perfectly is your work. In the human area you need more work here."

She could see herself trotting obediently off to the analyst twice a week until she got married, and then still "more work" at the analyst until she produced two children, a number the doctor found ideal for mental health, and then more sessions of "work" until she was safely living in the suburbs. It could take years!

"Do you think I'm going to commit suicide?" she asked.

He laughed. "No, not you."

"Do you think I'm going to become an alcoholic?"

"No."

"Do you think I'm a lesbian?"

"No."

"Then I think I'm going to work out the rest of my problems by myself," she said.

"But of course we must do a great deal of work by ourselves," he said indulgently. "I expect you to think between sessions. That is how we grow."

"No, I mean I'm quitting."

He seemed very angry. He half stood up in his chair. "You think you can just walk out and reject me?" he said. "I can do it to you, I can throw you out."

Her first thought was that he was testing her: how would she react to being sent away? But why would he do that? Then she thought he might really be upset, his face had reddened, and it occurred to her he might be a quack. To comfort him she told him she had to go to Europe, which was true, and said she would call when she returned.

She never called.

The first time she saw Rome, from her airplane seat, she felt as if she had come home. The odd terra-cotta colors of the city below amazed her. Her Italian was limited to what she had been able to cram from a small language book during the plane trip over the ocean, but she was not afraid. Even the language seemed musical and familiar. A magazine had sent her to interview Aldo Amico, movie star and sex symbol, and they had paid for the fare and given her enough money to stay two weeks, knowing he would be hard to trap. Carol had already written to her friend Luciana, who lived in Milan, and Luciana was going to meet her in Rome and had reserved her a room in a small hotel in Parioli, a short cab ride from the center of Rome, a hotel where American tourists never stayed and a good room with a balcony could be had for six dollars a day.

She supposed Luciana was her best friend. They had met the year before in Milan, and when Carol had left to go back to America, Luciana had cried. "I wonder if we will ever see each other again in this life," Luciana had said. She had never been to America.

Luciana's family was Sicilian. When she was a child, her mother would look at her down the length of the dining table fringed with her ten children and say: "You look like a black spider. Who will ever marry you?" By thirty Luciana had managed to find two husbands. The first she had married in a synagogue, so it was not considered legal in the Church and she had been able to divorce him, and the second was a Milanese aristocrat with a harelip and a great deal of money, who was in textiles and traveled. They had a "modern" marriage: she was free to travel too.

The black spider would never be pretty, but she was strange and beautiful, her skin silky, her hair blue-black (she used a blue rinse), the whites of her huge black eyes so clear, her teeth so white, her body perfect (she had a massage every day), her clothes impeccable, her jewelry dazzling. She had even become a painter of some note, making strange, haunted pictures, many of which featured spiders in a disguised form. This was before LSD.

Luciana met Carol at the airport and cried again. She was staying with a friend from Sicily, Little Lea, who had a house a block away from Carol's hotel. Carol was not sure whether Little Lea was Luciana's friend or a cousin; Italian family relationships confused her and Luciana sometimes made mistakes in English.

The three of them had dinner in an outdoor restaurant because it was summer. Little Lea looked like a kewpie doll, five feet tall, very curvy, with a round face full of winsome stupidity. She spoke no English but she went along amiably with anything the other two wanted to do.

"I want to get Aldo Amico right away," Carol said, "so I can get rid of him and see Rome."

"You have two weeks," Luciana said, "so we'll go to Capri too. I have a good friend, Marco, not a lover, he is coming here to meet me. His family owns half of Sicily. He will come with us."

Aldo Amico was filming at Cinecitta, and Carol had his home number too. The next two days she called him eight times, leaving messages with the housekeeper, and called the studio five times, but he was never available. She bought a small mozzarella and a bottle of red wine and had lunch on her balcony in the sun, looking at the rooftops and the bright blue sky, doubting that he would return her calls. Luciana came to get her in the afternoon.

"So?"

"I can't get to him yet."

"You are not clever," Luciana said. "Give me the number."

Luciana called Cinecitta and put her handkerchief over the mouthpiece of the phone. "Long distance from America," she said in Italian. She turned to Carol. "They're going to get him. No one can resist long distance from America." A moment later, Aldo Amico was on the line.

"This is Carol Prince," Carol said.

"Yes, I know," he said, sounding disappointed. "I

can't see you. I'm too busy. I'm making a picture and dubbing another at the same time."

"I can come over right now."

"I'm leaving in half an hour."

"I only need five minutes with you."

"Well, if I'm still here."

She ran out to the street and got a taxi. Luciana was looking very pleased with herself as she waved good-bye. At the studio Carol pushed her way through a troupe of extras, who all looked as if they were dressed like Julius Caesar, and found Aldo Amico just getting into his sports car. She sent the taxi away.

"I'm just leaving, you see," Aldo Amico said.

"I have no way to get back."

"Get in," he said. "I'll drive you back."

It was an open two-seater car and he drove almost a hundred miles an hour. She was terrified. But she knew she had him. A car was like the womb, they all talked there, feeling safe.

"I have nothing to say to you," he said. "I never discuss my private life."

"Of course not. It's all right."

Then he began to jabber about himself, his love affair with a notorious movie star, another with a princess, on and on, taking the roads like a hot-rodder. She had no pencil, no pad, she never took notes. They always felt safer that way, and she had an excellent memory. He pulled up at an apartment building.

"My house."

He got out of the car and she followed him. A middle-aged woman in black, wearing a white apron, opened the apartment door. She looked like the housekeeper, but Aldo Amico kissed her and called her Mama.

"A terrible woman reporter has been calling you for two days," the woman said in Italian. Carol understood her and laughed. The woman glanced at her, suddenly realizing, and left the room.

"My housekeeper," he said. "She protects me." Then he led Carol around the apartment, showing her things he had bought on his travels. He gave her a glass of wine, appraising her. "You are not what I expected," he said. "You are young and pretty."

"Thank you."

A slim young man came into the room. Aldo Amico spoke to him in Italian. "My bodyguard will drive you home," he said. "It is cold in my car. You can borrow my sweater." He took off his cashmere cardigan and put it over her shoulders.

"Thank you," Carol said.

"For what? I didn't say anything. It was not an interview. I told you, I never talk about my private life."

He shook her hand and she left with the bodyguard, who looked as if he couldn't defend anybody, but perhaps he had a gun.

In front of her hotel Carol tried to give the sweater to the bodyguard. "Please give this to Mr. Amico and say thank you."

"No, no. He will want to come for it himself." The young man smiled at her with pointed teeth, and she suddenly felt very seductive.

"Are you sure?"

"Of course."

But Aldo Amico never came for his sweater, nor did he call. It was an expensive sweater, but apparently he had either forgotten it or he felt it was a small price to pay for never having to see her again. It was her first lesson about celebrities and Carol was not really surprised. You didn't ever become friends with them from an interview. People who didn't know about her life thought she probably slept with all those sexy movie stars, and perhaps some interviewers did, but she doubted it. She was using him for her article and he was using her for publicity, and that was no basis for anyone to want to know someone better.

"The sweater of Aldo Amico!" Little Lea said at dinner. "What a souvenir!"

"It's too big," Carol said.

For the rest of the week she and Luciana saw all of Rome, sometimes accompanied by Little Lea. Luciana was waiting for Marco so they could go to Capri. At the end of the week the hotel manager saw Carol in the lobby and asked her to come into his office. He was a handsome young man who spoke English.

"You are a journalist," he said.

"Yes."

"I like journalists. You are on expense account?"

"Yes."

"I know about expense accounts." He smiled. He took her bill from his desk. "I like to help journalists. Your room is six dollars a day. I know your magazine pays for it. Now, I cannot lie, that would be dishonest, but our most expensive room is twenty-four dollars a day. So I will give you a bill for twenty-four dollars a day that you can give to your magazine, but you will be paying us six dollars a day, so that will be good for you. All right?"

Carol had a moment of confusion. No one had ever done this for her before. Did he expect her to split the difference with him? He seemed so innocent and pleasant, standing there smiling, that she doubted it.

"Well," she said, "thank you."

"It's nothing. I like journalists."

He handed her two hotel bills, one the real one, one the fake one. She smiled and thanked him again, and because he seemed to be through with her she left. Afterward she told Luciana.

"He didn't ask me to have a drink, he didn't try to come to my room, he didn't even ask me to mention his hotel."

"Of couse not," Luciana said. "We are a civilized country."

The next day Luciana took her shopping for clothes.

"Don't spend all your money," Luciana said. "You need some for Capri. But it's very cheap there. I know a hotel that's only two dollars a day. Tourists never heard of it. You get breakfast, too." She took Carol into a small upstairs shop. "It's very cheap here. Very chic. How old are you?"

"Twenty-seven," Carol said.

"You look forty. Where did you get those terrible clothes? In America?"

"Yes—"

"Give them to the maid. She will be very happy and love you forever. I never saw such styles. Americans must be crazy. And those shoes—clump, clump. Big American shoes. A woman's feet are very delicate, very sexy. Next we will get you some shoes. I don't know how American women can attract a man. American men don't know any better."

You could never argue with Luciana when she had decided to change someone's image, but you could never get angry with her either. She meant no malice. She was genuinely astonished that a woman would not try to be beautiful and sexy. So Carol let her pick out two dresses, two silk knit sweaters, a skirt, and later two pairs of shoes that hurt but looked very elegant. "It doesn't matter if they hurt," Luciana said. "You will get used to it."

Dressed in one of her new dresses and the new shoes, Carol went to Little Lea's house to meet Luciana for a drink. The maid opened the door cautiously, and then Luciana appeared in a housecoat, no makeup, and looking drawn.

"It's happening," she said.

From the bedroom there was a scream of pain—Little Lea. Luciana rushed into the bedroom, but Little Lea had gone into the bathroom where she was moaning. Luciana went into the bathroom. "Stay here," she said. "Don't look."

Carol sat on the edge of the unmade bed wondering what was going on. About ten minutes later Luciana came out of the bathroom supporting Little Lea, who was wearing a nightgown and looked deathly pale, perspiration on her face, circles under her eyes, her curly hair stringy.

"I think that was all of it," Luciana said. She spoke to Little Lea in Italian and helped her lie on the bed. The maid came in with a damp cloth to wipe Little Lea's face, and a bottle of wine and three glasses.

"The bidet was full of blood," Luciana said. "Clumps. I think the last one was the baby. I'm sure of it."

"What the hell's going on here?"

Luciana poured two glasses of wine and handed one to Carol. She said something to Little Lea, who shook her head. "She'll be all right in a little while. You see, it is very hard to get a divorce here in Italy. The only way is an annulment. Little Lea is married to a man she hates. It was an arranged marriage, for the money. She is very rich and so is he. In order to get an annulment she had to say to the Church that she never wanted to go to bed with a man again. It takes six years. Five years she waited, she had no lover, she never went to bed with a man. Next year she can get the annulment. But three months ago she went home to Sicily to visit, and there she went to bed with her cousin. She couldn't help it, she has been in love with him all her life, and five years without a man. . . . So of course she got pregnant. You see, if they found out she was pregnant, then she could not get the annulment. So today she went to a doctor. He did something to her to make her lose the baby. My God, I never saw so much blood." She said something to the maid in Italian, and the maid scurried out and returned with a glass jar. "Lea can show the doctor what came out," Luciana said. "But I'm sure it was the baby, it was so big. It's all so stupid. She should have waited. It was so soon now. But everything will be all right."

"Is she going to marry her cousin?" Carol asked.

"I don't know," Luciana said. "I think right now she hates him." She poured a glass of wine and gave it to Little Lea, speaking to her gently in Italian. Little Lea smiled and began to cry. Luciana made a face. "She loves him."

2

Carol went to Capri with Luciana and Marco. Their hotel was on a tiny curving street, her two-dollar room was huge and opened onto a garden filled with flowers where they had their free breakfast, and although the bathroom was infested with aggressive flies, she was surprised to find the first decent toilet paper she had ever seen in Europe.

Marco was not very tall, and terribly skinny, as if he had spent his childhood drinking wine instead of milk. But she found herself attracted to him. Perhaps because he was strange, perhaps because he was there. Every night she fantasized him coming to her room, wanting him. Perhaps he was Luciana's lover. Perhaps he had been. But the black spider surrounded herself with men who were not her lovers, just admirers, attracting them in some strange way that had nothing to do with her looks, using her marriage as an excuse to keep them out of her bed. Carol had seen Luciana at parties, the least beautiful woman there, and by the end of the evening surrounded by all the men in the room.

They went to the stony beach, they ate small shrimp by the sea, they all had sandals made, they strolled by the Hotel Quintiana at night to laugh at the tourists in their Pucci shirts and transparent plastic handbags. They had aperitifs in the town square at five o'clock and stared at the freaks, the rich old widows with their gigolos, the young girls with long straight hair and big sunglasses and their rich older men. Perhaps the freaks thought they too were freaks: an adventurous ménage à trois. Still, she wanted Marco to come to her room.

The three of them sat in the hotel garden having a coffee before going to bed. The last diners were still lingering over their coffees, the unadventurous guests who preferred to take their meals at the hotel. The air smelled of night-blooming flowers. Luciana rose. Carol started to get up too.

"No," Luciana said softly. "Never leave a man alone." She picked up her purse as if she were only going to the bathroom, and never came back.

"It is a beautiful night," Marco said.

"Yes."

"Capri is beautiful."

"Yes, it is."

"My country is beautiful too. You must come to visit me. It is a rough, dry land, but it is wonderful. I love it. I will take you to see everything. You will stay in my house. It is very big, with vineyards. You have been to Sicily?"

"No, never."

"You must come. It is restful. You can write there in peace."

"I would like that very much."

"I think Luciana has gone to sleep."

"I think so," Carol said.

"I will walk you to your room."

When they got to her room he came in. "I may stay?"

"Please do."

They undressed without a word.

"I'm sorry," he said when nothing happened.

"It's all right."

What could you say? Why hadn't anyone ever written advice on what to tell a man when he finds himself unable to make love? She ought to write an article about that, it would be so useful, but of course no one would touch it; magazines didn't admit such things happened.

Marco dressed and went back to his own room. She was not sorry to see him go; she really didn't know him well enough to want to sleep all night with him.

The next day she told Luciana. "He came to my room."

"I am not surprised. He likes you."

"Nothing happened."

"I could have told you that. I'm sorry."

"But if he knew, why did he try?"

"He still tries," Luciana said.

Marco came back to Rome with them, and when he left for Sicily he asked Carol again to visit him and gave her his address. She wondered what her analyst would have said about that. He probably would have told her to go, to try. See how Marco is always willing to try? A nice quiet place where you can write. A man with money, a nurse for the children—if there ever are any. Love can come later. Everyone is entitled to a mistake, don't judge a man by one night, maybe you're the one who can save him. At least you'll have a nice free trip.

She knew she would never go. It would be like a prison. Prisons were what she had been running away from all her life.

3

Carol went home to New York and wrote the article about Aldo Amico, which to her surprise was a great success. In himself, Aldo Amico was not interesting, but he was a mirror of the glamorous women he had made love to, and the world was interested in him. Carol's new clothes and shoes were a great success too, but the shoes never stopped hurting, and after a while they disappeared into the back of her closet to gather dust. The article was later bought from the magazine by a newspaper syndicate and run with many publicity photographs of Aldo Amico and his famous paramours, and Carol's agent was getting phone calls from magazines who wanted Carol Prince's name on the cover.

Her agent was now setting up business lunches where she accompanied him to fairly expensive, noisy restaurants and spent an hour watching him and whichever editor it was that day down several drinks, listened to them compare stories about their commuter trains, listened to some trade gossip over the heavy food they had ordered ("Grace Metalious will never write another book, John—we all know her husband wrote *Peyton Place*"), and then when they finally got to the coffee the editor would turn to her brightly and say: "Well, Carol, we certainly want you to write something for us."

"I'm not going to any more lunches," she told her agent one day in the office.

"Why not?"

"Because they're a waste of time. I'd rather sleep late. That little business we do, we can do on the phone."

"Business is meeting people," he told her. "Making friends."

"I still get the same dumb assignments. Advice to the lovelorn. How to get a man. How young girls go astray. And an occasional movie star. I want to do something important."

"Do what you're good at," her agent said.

"How do you know I wouldn't be good at something important?"

"You're not an economist. You're not a politician. You're not a man. What do you want to write about?"

"I certainly can't tell from reading those magazines I'm in. There's nothing there I wish I'd written."

"Magazines are for entertainment."

"There must be other magazines."

"Why do you want to go making trouble?" he said. "These editors are nice people. They love you. You can work all the time."

He's got me working steadily, she thought, and that's all he cares. She lit a cigarette.

"If you can think of an idea," he said, "tell me. I'll try to sell it."

She felt dismissed.

On her own she managed to talk a magazine into letting her do a piece on racing drivers (it wasn't important, but at least it was different) who were going to be at Monza, which was near Milan. She was glad of the unexpected chance to see Luciana again, and she was pleased with herself for getting the assignment because it was not the sort of assignment usually given to a woman. Her agent would never have thought of it. But she had told the editor she was a great expert on the subject, which was not true. She bought every motor racing magazine she could find, read them, and took them with her on the plane.

She stayed at a hotel in Milan, paid for by the magazine. They had also bought the plane ticket. There
were a great many press and photographers staying at
the hotel, as well as the drivers. It was an extraordinary
combination: the regular guests, old, staid, always
dressed for dinner, and the drivers in short-sleeved
sports shirts or sweaters, often with jeans, all having
aperitifs in the lounge while a string quartet played
classical music.

The drivers seemed to like her. It was like being back
in college again, talking to boys, asking them about
their favorite sport about which she knew nothing.
They thought she was funny because she had been
given this assignment knowing nothing about racing,
and they patiently explained everything to her. She
took notes, to look serious, although she always remembered everything. She had a press pass, a track pass,
and a pit pass, each encased in plastic and worn on her
nylon Goodyear jacket (a status symbol she had cadged
from one of the drivers), and the passes were to be
worn at all times. She would have worn them anyway;
they made her feel important.

One night she was in a restaurant in a cellar with a
group and realized that she was the only woman among
ten men. She was one of them. It was her childhood
dream come true, the girl reporter in a man's world,
the dream she had lingered over while her friends
were dreaming of going to Hollywood and being best
friends with Shirley Temple. The driver sitting next
to her had his hand on her leg, but it didn't matter
because none of the others knew it. She was no one's

mistress, she was an equal. The hand was warm and felt cozy, and he was pouring information into her ear, which was what was really important, even though he was trying to impress her because she was a girl. Let that ugly photographer across the table, Freddie the Frog Face, who was looking at her jealously, top that! Freddie was American, from the Bronx, and they had hated each other on sight, trading sharp quips like Katharine Hepburn and Spencer Tracy in one of those old movies about career girls. They would probably end up in each other's arms in the last reel.

Freddie was doing two jobs at once: the drivers and also a movie which was being made on location, some kind of love story with an international cast, marking the debut of Virginie, a young French folk singer. Virginie had a small part and spent most of her time sleeping on sofas and chairs like a lazy cat, bored because she spoke only French, her lover's wife had come to visit, and because even though her part was small the studio would not let her go home because they might need her for publicity. Freddie always spoke to her in English and she seemed to understand. At least he was the only person Virginie ever smiled at.

Carol had studied French in school and spoke it with an abominable accent. Every time she saw Virginie she said: "Hello, how are you?" and Virginie answered, sighing: "I'm so bored." Carol could never think of anything else to say to her, but she thought Virginie was one of the most beautiful girls she had ever seen, and she liked to look at her. Freddie evidently thought so too, he had taken hundreds of pictures of her.

The studio was going to charter a private plane to take the entire cast to the Venice Film Festival for publicity. Carol displayed her press pass and asked the unit publicist if she could go too, and he said of course. Luckily they were going several days after the race, as she had to cover it for her story.

She had never seen an auto race before. She knew by now how dangerous it was, but she had not expected to be so affected. There in the stands in the bright sun, with the international flags waving and the little bug-like cars flashing around the track making their aggressive noise, she suddenly found herself crying. In a few days these men had become her friends. One of them might be killed. *How can people watch this?* she thought. *They're just waiting for someone to die. I hate racing. I'm never going to another race.*

Then the car she had been rooting for did not appear for two laps. She knew what had happened. She ran down into one of the pits but no one knew yet exactly what had happened. A man went around the track on a motorcycle and reported that the driver had been killed. Then someone else came up and said he had only been hurt and the ambulance had gone to get him. Carol ran to the exit in time to see the ambulance still there. She looked so distrait that a man who seemed official tried to push her into the ambulance, speaking quickly to her in Italian.

"What did he say?" she asked a man standing there in the crowd.

"He says because you're the driver's wife you can go with them."

"No," she said, "I'm not his wife."

When the ambulance drove away without her she immediately regretted it. What a story, what a fool she was. Where were her instincts? She went back to the race, and that night she found out from one of the drivers that the injured driver had been flown to a hospital in London. She put through a long distance call to him there, and to her surprise she got through to him. He said he had only broken two ribs and would be racing again soon. She was the first one to know what had happened. But what was strange was that none of the driver's friends really seemed to care. They were so used to death, what was two broken ribs? One of them was permanently crippled and still drove in a specially equipped car so he could shift with his left hand.

"You're crazy," she told one of the drivers. "Why do you do this?"

"If I didn't, I'd still be a garage mechanic," he said. He wore Turnbull & Asser shirts and drank French champagne. He had a life insurance policy of a million dollars to go to his wife and children. She could not picture him as a garage mechanic anymore, although once he had been, in a grubby coverall, and he still stood around the garage supervising his troupe of mechanics. And if he was still a mechanic, he would not have been sitting in that cellar restaurant with his hand on the American reporter's leg.

The crash frightened the studio and the next day the unit publicist told the cast of the picture that the private plane to Venice had been canceled. They could not afford to lose the entire cast of a picture in the middle of shooting. The drivers had left to go on to their next race and the hotel seemed quiet and dull. Virginie came up to Carol in the lobby.

"I'm so disgusted," she said in French. "I bought a very expensive dress for the festival, and I had it shortened so now they won't take it back. Where am I going to wear it?"

"That's a shame," Carol said.

"It's not a dress I would ever wear to a party. I'm so angry." Virginie drifted away, not looking angry, just bored.

She was planning to move in with Luciana for a while, but the next morning Virginie came up to her in the lobby and said: "I'm so bored. Do you want to go to Venice? I have a car. We can go to the beach. I don't have to work for two days."

"All right."

"We'll leave from the hotel at five o'clock."

"What shall I bring to wear?"

"Just blue jeans. Maybe bring a dress. That's all."

She called Luciana to tell her she would be going to Venice for two days, packed her things, and checked out of the hotel. Luciana arrived in her car to take the suitcases to her apartment. Carol was wearing jeans and had rolled a dress into her shoulder bag along with some cosmetics and toilet articles. She could buy a bikini when she got to Venice. Virginie was in front of the hotel at five with a small, expensive-looking foreign car, a Val-pak, two suitcases, and a makeup box that looked like a mechanic's kit and was so heavy Carol could not lift it.

"All that for two days?"

Virginie smiled. "Do you want to see my dress?" She unzipped the Val-pak revealing a fantasy of sequins and feathers that must have cost hundreds of dollars. "A boy is coming with us. He asked for a ride."

The boy was Freddie, his frog face all innocence, cameras strung around his neck, a bag of flash bulbs and film in his hand.

"Oh, *you're* coming," he said.

"Same to you."

Virginie drove, Freddie sat in the back looking cheerful and being pleasant for once. They drove past famous places Carol had read about . . . Verona, the home of Romeo and Juliet . . . she wished they could stop. It was night when they got to Venice, and Virginie entrusted the car to the parking lot attendant and they managed to get all the gear onto the public ferry boat. Virginie insisted on paying their fares. When they reached the hotel the unit publicist was standing in the lobby. He looked horrified when he saw them.

"You came on the *public boat?*" he said to Virginie. "You shouldn't have done that, you're a star. I would have come to get you." Since he spoke in English she didn't understand him. She shrugged. "It's lucky we didn't give up all the rooms," he said. "There isn't a room in town. You wouldn't have had a place to stay."

He checked them in and they went to their rooms, arranging to meet later for dinner. They escaped the publicist and went to a small outdoor restaurant for pizza. Virginie insisted on paying for Carol and Freddie.

"Tomorrow we'll go to the Lido," Freddie said. "Are you coming, Carol?"

"What's there?"

"The festival. Stars. I'm going to take pictures."

"No," Carol said. "I've never been to Venice. I'm going to take a ride on a gondola."

She felt sorry for Virginie who looked so young sitting there in her jeans and long straight hair and no makeup, a star who carried a makeup case that must have weighed twenty pounds and wanted to take the public boat, who had asked her to come to Venice because she obviously had no friends. Perhaps she shouldn't leave her, even with Freddie. "Do you want me to go with you?" she asked Virginie.

Virginie shook her head and smiled.

"Is my French all right? Do you understand me?"

Virginie looked embarrassed. "I must tell you, please speak in English. I never understand a word you say."

"Never?"

"No, never."

Freddie laughed.

"Do you understand Freddie?" she said in English.

"Sometimes. Better than you."

"See, international sophisticate," Freddie said.

Virginie looked as if she didn't understand him either, but she smiled at them both in a sweet way, and Carol realized that if she had not asked, they would have gone on talking gibberish to each other forever, and it would not have mattered because people really didn't communicate with each other very often even when they spoke the same language. They just wanted the other people to be there.

The next morning Carol hired a gondola and toured the canals. It was like a movie. It was everything she had expected, but even better. Some of the canals smelled from garbage, and there was garbage in the water and even an old mattress, but it was Venice, and she was there. The gondolier had the decency not to sing.

Afterward she walked around and went to St. Mark's Square. There were beatniks sitting around the statue in the sun playing guitars, reading paperback books, smoking, or just sitting. They had backpacks and looked dirty, and she wondered if they slept around the statue at night. She watched them for a while and then she sat with them. They didn't seem to mind her because she was wearing jeans and sandals and her oversized shoulder bag looked a little like a backpack too. A fat girl wearing sunglasses smiled at her.

A boy handed the fat girl a joint, she inhaled deeply and handed it to Carol. Carol had never had one before but she knew what it was, slightly surprised it had gotten to Europe. She took a drag and handed it to the person next to her. The pot wasn't having any effect on her and she wondered why. It was pleasant there in the sun and she sat there for a long time watching the pigeons. It was a nice afternoon, no thoughts, no memories, no plans.

When Carol got back to the hotel, the unit publicist

was in the lobby again, talking to some people. That seemed to be his office.

"We're going to the opening tonight," he said to her. "We leave at seven o'clock. I have a launch. It's black tie."

"I didn't know that. I only have a short dress."

"Then you'll have to wear it. Nobody will be looking at you, anyway."

The dress had been hanging in the closet since her arrival and it was not wrinkled, but it looked singularly inappropriate. Still, it was better than blue jeans and she had nothing else. She took a shower and put on the dress, trying to pretend her shoulder bag was a camera case, and to further disguise herself as an intellectual journalist she put on her sunglasses. On the motor launch were the publicist, two other men, a woman, Virginie in her sequins and feathers, and Freddie with his cameras.

"What a great day we had!" Freddie said. "I took millions of pictures of Virginie. You should have come. Everybody was there."

"I had a great day, too. I've seen movie people, but I'd never seen Venice."

"Virginie was a great hit," Freddie said.

At the theater an American movie star was handed to Virginie, they shook hands, and then they entered the theater together while flashbulbs popped all around them. "Don't leave me," Virginie whispered to Carol, looking frightened.

As soon as Virginie and her date had gotten into the

theater, he said good-bye and dashed away through a side door. Virginie went to her seat alone.

"What was that all about?" Carol said to the publicist.

"He had to rush home to his wife."

Carol knew that the next day the American papers would be full of pictures of Virginie and her latest "romance." If that was all being a movie star got you, then it wasn't much.

The film was the usual American contribution to a foreign festival, showing that American youth were all no-good bums. It was greeted with warm applause. Afterward she found Virginie in the crowd in the lobby and Virginie took hold of her arm. "Don't leave me."

"I won't."

When Carol and Virginie emerged from the theater, a crowd of what seemed at least five hundred people came rushing at them, screaming: "Virginie! Virginie!" Carol had had no idea Virginie was so famous. Virginie was pale and shaking. The crowd looked crazy, as if it was going to run right over them, arms outstretched, mouths open, howling their greed and love. They're going to trample us to death, Carol thought. They're going to kill us. But she felt strangely calm. She stood there at the top of the marble stairs and held up her hand like a traffic cop. The crowd stopped dead and looked at her. She supposed she was an odd sight among all those people in their formal clothes and jewels and elaborate coiffeurs, a frump in a short cotton dress with sunglasses and a huge leather pouch hanging from her shoulder; a tough lesbian, a meter maid, someone Official. I am Official, she told herself, and led Virginie quickly through the space the crowd cleared for her until they were safely away and surrounded by the publicist and his friends.

"Who the hell is she?" one of the men whispered to the publicist, looking at Carol.

"A journalist."

"Oh."

They went to a party at the big hotel on the Lido. Carol sat at a table with the publicist and his friends and Virginie. Freddie was nowhere to be seen, off taking pictures of stars. They drank bellinis, and Carol realized the man who had asked about her was sitting next to her. He seemed to be American. He also seemed pleasant, but she didn't like his hair, combed back with some sort of goo like Elvis Presley, and besides, she hadn't come here to meet Americans.

Afterward on the motor launch she realized that she could not bear to leave Venice the next day. Virginie was asleep. The wind was blowing the American's hair and he looked much better than he had at the party.

"You speak English?" she said to him.

"Yes, of course. I've been talking to you all evening."

"Oh, that was you."

"Yes, I'm American."

"What's your name?"

"Eric. What's yours?"

"Carol."

The lights flickering on the water were so beautiful. Venice! She couldn't leave so soon. "Are you staying a while?" she asked Eric.

"A few days."

"Are you alone?"

"Yes," he said.

"Do you want to play with me?" His face lit up. "No, I don't mean it that way," she said. "I mean do you want to sight-see and stuff?"

"Sure."

"Freddie can drive back with Virginie," Carol said to the publicist.

"No, I'm staying a few days to cover the festival," Freddie said.

"Well, someone ought to drive back with Virginie. I don't want her to drive alone. She's too tired. Can you give her a driver?"

"Don't worry about it," the publicist said. "I'll send someone with her."

Virginie woke up.

"Do you mind?" Carol asked her.

She shrugged. "No."

"Are you sure?"

"Yes."

In the lobby Carol gave Eric her room number, and he said he would come to get her at ten the next morning. Freddie gave her an evil grin. She kissed Virginie good-bye and went to the elevator. Freddie rode up with her because their rooms were on the same side.

"So she got to wear her dress here after all," Carol said.

"Yup," Freddie said. "Virginie's very smart."

4

Eric came to get her at ten o'clock the next morning.
He took her to the Biennale, which was supposed to be
an art show but looked more like a bad world's fair.
They went to several pavilions, remarked how funny
the pictures were, and then sat in a small park drinking
zambucas and talking. She learned he was thirty-four,
an unsuccessful agent, had a wife in Rome, where he
was temporarily living, had no children, and had gone
to the festival to find new clients, but mainly to get
away from his wife. Since he showed no inclination to
return to the festival, and Carol was not an actress, she
could see why his business was not doing well. They
played tag around the statues, saw some more paintings,
and then went to a restaurant where he bought her
lunch. After lunch they walked, stopping at stalls to
buy useless souvenirs, looking at people, getting lost,
and finally ending up in St. Mark's Square where they
had coffee at an outdoor cafe. Carol looked among the
kids at the statue, but the fat girl was no longer there.

"Crazy beatniks," he said.

"Why do you wear your hair like that?"

"Like what?"

"All slicked back like Elvis Presley."

"I like it."

"Oh."

"You don't?"

"No."

"Well, I do."

"Okay."

She also didn't like his pinkie ring, but she figured she had said enough for one day. She liked other things about him. He could be handsome, he was sweet, and they had a good time together. She was lucky to have found someone to play with in Venice so quickly, because that was what one wanted, a beautiful foreign city to explore and a lover. She supposed he would be her lover soon.

After dinner he came to her room with her quite naturally, looking a little shy, and they went to bed. His hair was all curly when it got messed up and made him look like a statue of a Greek god. She was really annoyed with him for being so stupid about his hair. If they could just stay in bed together forever, she would like him much better.

"You're beautiful," she told him.

"I love you," he said.

It was an amenable thing to say and seemed appropriate for the circumstances, so she said: "I love you, too."

The next morning he went to his room to shower and change and then they went sight-seeing again. She did not see Freddie anywhere, which was odd. She supposed he was working. She wanted Eric to take her to dinner at a rooftop restaurant she had seen in that movie about the old maid who went to Venice and found love, so he did. She liked knowing she would never be like the pathetic woman in that picture.

When they finished dinner Eric was rather drunk, and when they got to her floor he ran up and down the halls rearranging all the pairs of shoes in front of the wrong rooms. Poor innocent, trusting tourists, putting their shoes out at night to be polished. In New York somebody would probably steal them.

"Don't do that," she said.

"Why not?" he said, laughing.

"They'll blame the hotel."

"Imagine their faces in the morning! We'll have to get up early so we can hear them scream."

"Let's go to bed," she said. Why were men such little boys?

She really did like him better in bed. Bed was an oasis. She liked the room, it was so old-fashioned. He had a beautiful body, and she was relieved he had put the pinkie ring on the dresser when he undressed. Clothes and hair and jewelry categorized people too much, like what they did for a living and where they had gone to school. In bed you could be tender to a real person. They kept waking up during the night and looking at each other. This was partly romantic and partly because the bed was too small for comfortable sleep. They both chose to think of it as romantic. He told her again that he loved her, and she replied that she loved him, too. After all, she didn't know what love was, so there was no harm in it, and she did like him.

The next morning she phoned Luciana to tell her

she had met a man and would be staying a few more days.

"Always a lover," Luciana said, pleased. "Call me when you come back."

They spent five days in Venice in all. It was just enough; more would have been boring. The weather was turning cloudy. They went back to Milan on the train.

"Don't you have to go to Rome to work?" she said.

"I can see some clients in Milan."

"I'm going to have to work when I get there."

"That's all right," he said. "As long as I come first."

He had taken a room at the hotel where she had stayed and insisted she come up to see it. Then he insisted they go to bed. She was impatient to see her friends, and annoyed at him. She didn't feel sexy.

"My wife will kill me," he said happily. "I haven't even called her."

"You should call her."

"No, no, then she'll scream that I should come home."

Downstairs in the lounge where people had drinks she saw Freddie. She was surprised how glad she was to see him. "When did you get back?"

"Today. And you?"

"Just now. Where were you in Venice?"

"I met a girl."

"Ah." He and Eric shook hands, and Freddie gave her another of his evil grins. "We're having dinner at some restaurant with my friend Luciana and her husband," Carol said. "Why don't you come?"

"Okay."

At the restaurant there were Luciana, her husband,

Bruno, who liked Carol, two business associates of Bruno's, and Freddie and Eric. Luciana looked glamorous and was charming to Eric and Freddie. It was a Chinese restaurant because Bruno loved Chinese food.

"This reminds me of a Chinese whorehouse I went to several times in Hong Kong," Eric said. "What beautiful girls! They know everything to do to please a man. There are no girls in the world like those Chinese whores." He launched into a boring anecdote and Freddie rolled his eyes and kicked Carol under the table. Luciana listened with the rapt attention she gave to all men.

After dinner they walked to Luciana's house. "Aren't you coming to the hotel with me?" Eric whispered.

"No," Carol said. "I'm staying here. I have to work."

"I came here to be with you."

"You said you came here to work. I'll see you tomorrow."

Eric came in and they all had drinks. Carol went into the kitchen. Freddie was there finding a Coke; he didn't like to drink.

"He's horrible," Freddie said. "Get rid of him."

"What's wrong with him?"

"That story about the whorehouse. He's a moron and a bore. That hair. That pinkie ring. That suit. He's too stupid for you. What did he do, follow you here?"

"I guess so."

"Well, send him back."

"You're just jealous. He happens to be a fantastic lay."

Finally at midnight Luciana announced she was

throwing everyone out. The two businessmen had long since left. "Come with me," Eric said to Carol.

"I can't."

"Yes, you can."

"No. I'll see you tomorrow."

Eric left with Freddie.

"That ugly one," Luciana said, "he is your lover too?"

"No, I just know him."

"I like him. He is intelligent. But that Eric, he is—"

"A porkeria," Bruno finished, smiling like a rabbit with his harelip.

"What's that?"

"Oh, it means some kind of garbage," he said.

"Nobody likes him?"

"But he's nothing," Luciana said. "Do you know what he did when you went to the toilet? He told everyone he was in love with you. He doesn't even know us."

"I think that's rather sweet."

"No," she said. "Not sweet. Drunk."

The next day Carol told Eric she had to go out of town for an interview at Luciana's husband's textile mill, and the day after when he called three times the maid said she had still not returned. At the end of the week he went back to Rome. Carol felt sorry for him but she could not think of any other way of handling it.

She received a letter from Eric: *Guess what happened when I got home. My wife had moved out bag and baggage. She even took the Crest! I've bought some more Crest, but I miss you. Can I come back and get you?*

She wrote back: *Please don't come. I need time to think.*

All her life she had been taught that it was the other way around: people met and had brief affairs, then they parted and the woman was the one who fell in love. The man wasn't supposed to fall in love. Eric hardly even knew her. Didn't he know the rules?

She was very relieved to find out much later that his wife had come back, they were reconciled, and they had decided to have a baby.

5

It was never difficult coming back to New York in the beginning; there was a piece to be written, work to be done. But after a week or two Carol always began to feel that New York, not the European city she had left, was the foreign country, for it was here that she felt like a stranger. New York was her home and she could not imagine living anywhere else, but people always made her feel as if there was something wrong with her because she was not like them. She and Freddie had exchanged phone numbers when they left Italy, deciding they might work together when the chance arose, and when he called her occasionally to say hello she felt as if he was a good friend. They were no longer mean to each other. He felt like a stranger here, too. He traveled often for his work, and wherever he went there always seemed to be a girl in love with him. Carol supposed they thought he led a glamorous life.

She would be thirty soon. Her only unmarried friend was Ellen, who was twenty-three and worked for Carol's agent. Ellen shared a crowded apartment with three roommates, they all had a lot of dates and there was no privacy. Everyone put her name on her own food in the refrigerator. Ellen was in no hurry to get married, but she was making elaborate plans to lose her virginity. Carol thought it was about time. The sort of boys Ellen dated were her own age and lived with their parents. There was one she had a crush on. For a month she made tentative plans to borrow Carol's apartment for a few hours, and finally she set the date on a Saturday afternoon. Carol put a bottle of champagne into the refrigerator, clean towels in the bathroom, clean sheets on the bed, put the key under the doormat and went to the movies.

After the movie she killed some time at the grocery stocking up for the following week, and came home when it was dark. It was obvious no one had been there. She called Ellen.

"What happened?"

"I chickened out."

They set two more dates and both times Ellen was too afraid to go through with it. Carol figured before a year was out Ellen would probably marry somebody. Girls like that did. You couldn't hold out forever, you had to make connection with someone one way or another. Carol opened the champagne and drank it herself.

She wondered why she didn't want to get married. People always asked her why. Her mother said that was a compliment and she shouldn't get annoyed; after all, if she were repulsive, people would know she'd never had the chance. Her friends told her that when you were thirty you went into a panic. She couldn't think of a worse panic than having to promise to belong to someone. She hated having to lie to all those strangers who asked her at parties and on dates: "Why haven't you ever married?" Ever, as if she were a hundred. As if she should invent a tragic divorce at twenty and the mandatory baby being cared for by her parents in the country because she was too immature. She hated having to pretend to strangers that she was anxious to get married, that she was looking, in order to prove that she liked sex and there was nothing wrong with her. Men were always allowed excuses: they were having too much fun being single, they were concentrating on their careers, they couldn't afford to support a family yet. Her mother told her about a girl they knew who was married; she had rich parents and they had given her a fur coat for Christmas. The husband had made her send it back to them. He wouldn't let her have anything he couldn't pay for himself. Everyone thought he was admirable except the girl's parents and Carol. Carol thought he was a shit.

Carol had bought a television set. That was the winter she went through what she thought of as her television mania. Her friend Billy, who was flagrantly gay, was an old movie nut. He liked to think he was Bette Davis. He knew every famous line from every one of her old pictures. He had a color set. Every day they read *TV Guide* and exclaimed with joy over what wonder would be on that night, especially if it was in color. Then if Carol didn't have to work she would be at his apartment, eating a Mexican TV dinner right out of the foil tray, rapt in front of the set. Sometimes Billy had some friends there, strange young men with plucked eyebrows. If she wanted to stay home, he would be on the phone during every commercial, shrieking with joy over what they had just seen. If he'd had his way, he would have kept her on the phone during the program as well, pretending they were watching it together. She had never really watched television before— most of the people she knew liked to say it was just for stupid people and would not admit they wasted time on it—and she devoured television watching with the same lust she might have given to studying history or art or a new hobby. If you had watched a soap opera, that was an extra credit, and if you had ever come home from a party at five in the morning and stayed up to watch Farm News, that was an A+. The best old movie on the Late Show was, of course, one you had seen before, so you could anticipate the lines that would make you collapse in joyous laughter. Billy was between jobs, so he had a lot of time to watch the afternoon movies on TV. He filled her in on what she had missed.

It was a phase, and Carol found it comforting. She resented the occasional dates she felt compelled to accept, because the movie she was missing seemed more real than the conversation over drinks with someone who seemed to be talking to himself. She preferred Billy's shrieks and manic laughter, even though she was always aware of the sadness under it. Everyone who tried could become an expert at something: Billy was an expert at passing time.

"I want to meet intellectuals," she told Freddie on the phone. "I'm supposed to be an intellectual, but I don't know any. I'm getting too attached to 'As The World Turns' lately."

"I'm going to cover a party tonight," Freddie said. "I'll take you. Everybody will be there, all the people from *The Paris Review*, magazine and book people, Andy Warhol. Ten o'clock."

The party was in a gallery which looked more like a barn because they had taken all the paintings away and covered the walls with aluminum foil. It was very dark, and colored lights traveled around the walls and on the faces of the guests. There was a loud rock band. Some of the guests looked as if they had come to a costume party, trying to outdo each other in flamboyant weirdness, but there were many intellectual-looking men in brown tweed suits and short haircuts. They all looked very tall. Carol felt short, particularly because people kept shoving her as if she weren't there. Freddie ran off immediately and she caught a glimpse of him from time to time, snapping pictures, ducking and lunging with amazing speed. He really was a pro.

She smiled at a few men but no one spoke to her. There was a long table set up along one wall with drinks and glasses. She got herself a drink, but someone immediately bumped into her and spilled it, rushing away without bothering to apologize. She wondered what was wrong with her; did she look so ugly, was she so unimportant? She had never been so ignored at a party before, but the parties she usually went to were given by someone she knew who introduced her to people. She saw Andy Warhol hiding shyly in a corner and felt better. No one was speaking to him either, but she could understand that; they were in awe of him, he was a celebrity. She, apparently, was just an unattached female, and not an Intellectual.

She decided on the man she found the most attractive, and smiled at him a few times, but he did not speak to her. Some nights she might have felt aggressive enough to speak to him, but tonight she felt rather put down. No one was really paying attention to anyone. They were paying attention to themselves.

In the center of the room she saw a very beautiful girl who looked like a model. She was six feet tall, as tall as the group of admiring men who surrounded her, and she had thick, shoulder-length blond hair that shone in the colored lights, first pink, then blue, heavy false eyelashes, a chiseled face, and was very thin, like a model. She was wearing a black jumpsuit and white gloves, like Minnie Mouse. Something about her seemed familiar. Carol wondered if she was a movie star. She went closer to the group and stood on the fringes of it, watching the men performing their courting ritual, hoping that one might decide he was outnumbered and notice her. None of them did.

There were some women you simply could not compete with. Carol knew she was attractive, but she also knew she was not the kind of woman men would walk across a room to meet. They would have to meet her first and then get to like her. It would be nice to be tall and skinny and blond, but if she were she would not wear white cotton gloves. The girl was obviously a hick.

Then the girl saw her, pushed through the circle of men with a shriek, and embraced her. For the first time the men turned and looked at Carol.

"Carol! It's me—Natasha."

Good God. Natasha was a skinny boy Carol had met one night sitting around Billy's apartment watching color TV with them. He had been wearing nylon stockings under his jeans and had given her the recipe for homemade bread. When Carol had asked him his real name he wouldn't tell her; he'd said it was an awful name, worse than Ignatz. Now he was wearing a wig, and she realized why he had on the white gloves; his hands were man's hands, heavily veined.

Natasha pulled Carol over to the corner, beyond earshot of her admirers. "Three of them asked me for my phone number," she said. "That one wants me to have dinner with him." She pointed at the man Carol had been yearning over all evening. "He's a publisher."

"Oh," Carol said.

"I don't know what to do," Natasha said. "I'd love to go out with him. I never met a publisher before, and he's really sexy, don't you think? But he thinks I'm a girl, and if he finds out, I'm afraid he'll beat me up."

"Do you really think he'll beat you up?"

"That's what I live in dread of," Natasha said. "It's hell on my social life. You can imagine how insulted his male pride would be to find out he'd been out with a boy."

"Natasha!" the men were calling impatiently. "Natasha! Come back!"

Natasha giggled. "Come with us, Carol. We're all going to some man's house for a party."

"I can't. I have a date."

"Bring him."

So this was beauty. So these were values. So here were her envied intellectuals. She wasn't going to go to the party and hang around waiting for a drag queen's leftovers. The attractive publisher came over and took Natasha's hand.

"Do you mind if I take your friend away?" he said to Carol, and led Natasha off.

Carol looked around until she saw Freddie. She had to run to catch him before he disappeared again.

"I'm going home now," she said. "Do you mind?"

"No, I have to stay and work. Aren't you having a good time?"

"No."

6

The next afternoon, seeking normalcy, she went to see her friend Bernice, who was married to a businessman and had three little children. She and Bernice had gone to high school together; Carol had been a bridesmaid. She brought an advance copy of a magazine where her latest article appeared.

Bernice was surrounded by French provincial furniture, flower-sprigged slipcovers, and bedlam. There were toys strewn on the living room floor, a stew was simmering on top of the kitchen stove, and there were stains on the rug. Carol gave her the magazine.

"There's a piece here I wrote."

Bernice leafed through the magazine greedily, not looking for the article. "Ooh, clothes!" she said. "I haven't seen any decent clothes for ages."

"It's on page fifty-two."

"I'll read it later. I'm too busy."

"How's everything?"

"All right. My mother-in-law is coming to dinner so I have to drag out the hideous silver she gave us. Do you want a drink?"

Carol followed her into the kitchen. Bernice made drinks and brought a bowl of dip and some celery into the living room, putting them on the coffee table. The oldest child was in his bedroom with the television on full blast, the middle one was running around the living room, and the youngest was rummaging through Carol's purse. Carol took a gulp of her vodka and tonic and discovered it was gin. She tried to retrieve her purse from the baby.

"Go potty," Bernice said calmly. "Go on, go potty, Cybill."

The baby wandered out of the living room with Carol's compact clutched in her fat hand.

"I went to this really weird party last night," Carol said.

"Don't tell me about parties, I'll get too jealous. We never go anywhere. The last time we went to the theater it was when I was carrying Cybill, and the water broke in the seat. My mother-in-law nearly fainted."

The four-year-old had discovered the dip and was putting his hands in it and smearing it on the couch. Bernice ignored him. "You'd better eat it before it's gone," she said.

Carol took a piece of celery. "Do you know any men for me?" She didn't know why she'd said it; it was just one of those things you said to your married friends.

"Are you kidding? Everybody we see is married. I never see anybody interesting anymore. I thought you must know millions of men."

"Nobody I like," Carol said.

"Well, you wouldn't like anybody I know. You can have Edgar—remember him? He's still single."

"No thanks."

"Remember Edgar?" Bernice said, smiling dreamily. "He used to send me all those roses. And I used to break my date with him every time Hank called. Hank knew about Edgar, of course, but Edgar never knew about Hank. He was really upset when I got married. Do you know, he still calls my mother to see how I am?"

"You would never have married Edgar."

"I used to think about it. But I couldn't stand to have him touch me. He'd be a good catch for some girl, though. He's awfully rich."

"Don't look at me."

"No, you can do a lot better than Edgar."

The baby toddled proudly into the room, holding her potty in both hands. There was a tiny turd in it.

"Good Cybill!" Bernice cried. "Good girl! Look, Carol, look at what Cybill did!"

Cybill smiled happily and brought the potty to Carol.

"Good girl," Carol said dutifully.

"You can take it away now," Bernice said. "Mommy's good, wonderful girl, take it back now."

Cybill put the potty unsteadily on the coffee table next to the dip her brother had demolished, and fell down. Bernice ignored it and began leafing through the magazine.

"I guess you can't have everything," Bernice said.

7

"Now, don't get mad," her mother said on the phone. "Hear me through. This is a man you might find interesting. He just got divorced. I understand it wasn't his fault—his wife was a little, well, unbalanced. He's a little old for you; he's forty-one, but he's supposed to look very young and he's an avid golfer. He's an executive. He's very well-to-do. Just meet him. You might have an interesting time, and he might have some nice friends."

"If he likes me he's not going to give me his nice friends."

"Just meet him. My friend Roberta, you remember her, her daughter is married to a doctor and has two children? She gave him your number."

"You've never seen him?"

"Now, how could I see him? He's a friend of Roberta's daughter's husband."

"Why didn't you ask me first?"

"You don't have to marry him," her mother said. "Just take a look at him."

The man called that evening. His name was William.

"I have a dinner date," he said, "but I could come to your apartment at eleven o'clock for a drink."

"I go to sleep at ten," Carol said.

"Well, then, the next time I'm free is next Friday."

"All right, I'll meet you somewhere about five."

"I'll come to your apartment. I think that's much nicer, don't you? Then we can have dinner afterward if you're free."

"I really don't mind meeting you somewhere."

"No, no," he said. "Give me your address."

"I hope you don't drink anything exotic," she said. "Scotch."

When she opened the door for William at five o'clock on Friday afternoon, Carol realized he would never see forty-one again. She doubted if he remembered being fifty. He had a reasonably good build, but his hair was obviously dyed and his teeth left much to be desired. She could see the small broken veins under the skin of his face. He was freshly shaved and smelled of pine cologne.

She made drinks and brought them into the living room. He was still standing, waiting to see where she would sit. She sat on the chair. He sat on the couch next to the chair, leaning so far forward she thought he was going to fall on the floor. She found herself cringing into the corner of the chair.

"This is a very nice apartment," he said. "May I see it?"

"This is it."

"No, there must be more."

Dutifully she rose and let him follow her. "This is

the kitchen. This is the bathroom. This is the bedroom."

He went into the bedroom, she stayed in the doorway.
He looked at her queen-size bed with approval.

"Nice bedroom."

She led him back to the living room and returned to
her chair.

"How long have you lived here?" he said.

"I don't know, about eight or nine years. It's rent
controlled."

"You've never married?"

"No."

"And I understand you're a writer."

"Yes."

He looked at her carefully. "What do you want to do
with your life?"

"I want to be a writer."

"No, I mean your life. What do you want to do? Who
do you want to be?"

"A person."

"Don't be flip with me."

He gave her the stern look a much older man gives
a young girl. She decided she definitely was not going
to have dinner with him. "Would you like some more
ice?"

He looked at his glass. "All right. And some scotch."

She got up to take his glass and he rose swiftly and
grabbed her around the waist. She slid away from him
and took his glass to the kitchen where she made him a
very weak drink.

"Tell me about your business," she said.

"It's very stimulating. I enjoy it. I work hard, but that's a good thing, I think. I'd rather talk about you."

"Well, I enjoy my work too."

"No, I mean you as a person. How old are you?"

"Thirty."

"Thirty. You don't look thirty. You could pass for . . . twenty-four, no, twenty-six. I don't see any gray hairs. You look very well for thirty. Some women fall apart, disintegrate, but you haven't. But you never know, you might. What are you going to do when you're forty?"

"Have a birthday party."

He leaned forward and took her hand. His hand was soft, an old man's hand, but when she tried to disengage it she discovered his grip was like steel.

"You're breaking my hand," she said.

He let go. "You have a good time, I suppose," he said. "Admirers, parties, lovers. I assume you have great sex. But what are you going to do when you're forty and alone?"

"I'll worry about it then."

"And fifty? What about when you're fifty?"

"You know," she said in a soft, vague voice, "people always refer to a Dirty Old Man, but you never hear them say a Dirty Old Woman. Women have more dignity. They learn to develop charm for when their youth and looks are gone. Women always lie to men; they tell them they're attractive and sexy when they really mean they're successful. Men believe them. But women don't lie to themselves. We're experts at looking in the mirror."

"I suppose I'd better be on my way," he said.

"Roberta says he said you were very bright," her mother said the next morning when she phoned.

"That was very civilized of him."

"Did you make another date with him?"

"No."

"But I suppose he'll call?"

"I don't think so."

"Why not?"

Carol didn't answer.

"Carol, you've always been very bright," her mother said. "I always knew you were bright. You got good marks in school. But sometimes men don't like a girl who's *too* intellectual."

"Mother!" Carol screamed. "Why doesn't anybody ask me if *I* liked *him?*"

8

Carol and Luciana seldom wrote to each other. Although Luciana could speak English she could not write it, and she had that strange handwriting Italians have which Carol could not decipher. Whenever she wrote to Luciana, she wrote: Please type!!! but Luciana apparently could not type either. So when Carol got an assignment to go to the north of England to do a piece on horse racing and jockeys, she was glad not only because she would be able to get away from New York but because she could fly to Italy afterward and meet Luciana. She wrote to Luciana before she left, but got no answer, which did not surprise her very much. When people were really good friends they could be casual about plans.

This new assignment gave her a few things to worry about. A movie was being shot about the racing, and the movie company was paying for her trip, but the piece was supposed to be mainly about the sport of racing, with the movie plugs fitted in subtly. The magazine was firm about not being used to publicize movies; still it could not afford to send her to England so it had to be realistic about what she had to do. She hoped the movie publicists would be equally realistic, not that they would see the piece until it was printed, but because she wanted future assignments.

Luckily there was a stretch of beautiful weather. She had always heard England was cold and damp, but it was greener than anything she had ever seen, and the sun shone every day, which everyone told her was unusual. There were two hotels in the small town. Carol was in the better one, along with the director, stars, hairdresser, makeup people with their equipment, including hair dryers, publicity staff, and the other reporters. The crew, secondary players, and the jockeys the studio had hired were in the bad hotel. They had also hired a lot of horses, who stayed in the stables and had the same status as the hired jockeys and secondary players. When there was no race the company shot around the track, stables, and grandstand, and when there was a race they filmed it and worked it into the footage.

There were a few wives, girl friends, and leftover one-night stands, but Carol was the only woman allowed everywhere at all times, except for the director's wife, who stayed away because she didn't like the smell. It was near the end of shooting, which was convenient for Carol because no one was nervous anymore, most of them were very bored, and it made them easier to talk to. The men, most of whom could not afford to have their wives or girl friends with them, were very horny after all that time, which made them most eager to talk to her, buy her drinks, and try to find out her room number. She enjoyed this, but none of them attracted her, and at night she always went to her room alone to write up her impressions.

All the other journalists were men, and none of them seemed to feel any guilt about spending the movie company's money; when it got too dark to shoot, they all met in the hotel suite which had been set aside as a press room and drank bottles of champagne, taking turns signing the bills with their room numbers, knowing all the checks were going to the same place. The unit publicist was a nice guy who encouraged this, saying: "Order Dom Perignon. Fuck 'em." He also bought them presents. Carol was a welcome member of the group. At first she was surprised at the way they were all wasting money, but then she realized that compared to the overall budget, what they were spending was nothing.

Peter Lugosi was the director. He went around telling people he was only half Jewish, when nobody had asked. He didn't like Carol because she was a woman and that had convinced him she was only there to write secrets about the sexual aberrations of his stars. She told him she was really there to find out whether they doped the horses, but he still didn't trust her.

Atalanta Brook was playing the second female lead. She had been married just before they went on location, and her husband was in New York where he was a stockbroker. She kept asking Carol to have lunch and dinner with her, and running over to her on the set whenever she wasn't working to ask her to have tea. Carol realized that Atalanta had decided that when she had finished being her Best Friend, the piece was going to be about her.

"It's wonderful being married," Atalanta said to her during one dinner. "My husband is a real man. He doesn't let me get away with anything. Whenever I'm a brat he turns me over his knee and spanks me."

Every day Atalanta said: "Be careful what you write about me, you will, won't you? This picture could do a lot for me." Carol didn't have the heart to tell her that if she was lucky the best she would get would be a still of her on a horse.

Every morning Carol got up at seven, which she hated, so she could get a ride to the track with the other reporters. She had still not decided what her approach to the piece would be, and it made her a little nervous. Peter Lugosi kept asking her what the piece was about and she didn't know. He also kept asking her when she was going home, and she didn't know that either. She rather envied the reporters with the tape machines who did a couple of interviews and then left. It was so much eaiser for them. But she was getting paid more than they were.

One evening they all got into cars and vans and drove out to a castle in the country for a party scene. Atalanta asked her to come; it was her big emotional scene and she said she was scared. Carol thought it might be exciting, and besides, she had never seen a castle, so she went. It was cold and damp. They would be shooting all night with a dinner break at about eleven. Carol sat on the back flap of the prop truck and drank scotch out of a paper cup, partly to keep warm and partly to hide from Peter Lugosi, who seemed more nervous than usual.

They finished the party scene with the extras, broke for dinner, and then the extras cleared out because it was time for Atalanta Brook's big emotional scene. She was on the driveway in a party dress, the lights were set up around her, the hairdresser took the clips out of her hair and sprayed it one last time. The camera with the man sitting on it hung over them, dark and quiet like just another one of the big trees on the drive. Then there was a fracas.

Lugosi was trying to pour scotch down her throat, and she was screaming that she didn't drink.

"I never had a drink in my life," she screamed.

"Shut up," he said. "You're supposed to be drunk."

"I can act drunk."

"You can't if you've never been drunk."

"Are you telling me I'm not an actress?"

"I'm telling you you're not that good an actress."

He tried to get her to drink from the bottle, but she coughed and turned her head away, so Lugosi got a paper cup from the prop man, poured a big belt of scotch into it, and shoved it into her hand. "Drink!"

She sipped and retched. He held the cup so she couldn't get it out of her mouth and she drank it all, then he filled it up again.

"I'm going to throw up," she screamed.

"Drink it."

When she finished the second cup of scotch, they ran through the scene several times and she was not very good. "Cut," Lugosi said. "More scotch."

He got that down her too, and she did the scene again a few times, and she seemed worse if anything. By now she was quite drunk and crying. "Good," he said. "Keep crying."

"I have to pee," she screamed.

"Pee in your pants. Roll it again."

By now he had her crawling on the driveway, grabbing bits of gravel and screaming out her lines with tears and dirt on her face, hysterical. Carol thought it looked like corny overacting. At this point there was a small crowd watching them because it was the first interesting thing that had happened all night. When they cut, Carol joined the crowd and Lugosi looked up and saw her.

"Get out of here," he said.

"I want her here," Atalanta said.

"This is a closed set. Get out."

"She asked me here."

"I wouldn't let Lillian Ross on a closed set, why should I let you. Get out."

She didn't move. She didn't have a ride home.

"She's my best friend, I want her to stay. I won't do the scene unless she stays," Atalanta screamed, very drunk and crying again.

Lugosi came over to Carol. "Listen here," he said quietly. "I don't care what you print. You can print anything you want."

"I wouldn't print this," Carol said. "My readers aren't interested in this. They're interested in the horses."

Then she went back to the prop truck and drank some more, but she couldn't seem to get warm or even drunk. Atalanta finished the bottle of scotch, did the scene a few more times worse than ever, finally did pee in her pants, and got completely hysterical and threw up. They got a doctor who gave her a shot and then they put her into someone's car and took her back to the hotel. Carol hitched a ride with some strangers.

When she got to the hotel the doctor was in the lobby, and he said that he had given Atalanta a sedative and she would sleep through the night. He asked if anyone else wanted a sedative but no one did. Carol went to her room, took two sleeping pills, and got into bed. The phone rang.

"Come to my room," Lugosi said. "I want to talk to you."

"I just took two sleeping pills and I'm in bed. If you want to talk to me you'll have to do it on the phone."

"Listen," he said, "your friend Atalanta isn't such an innocent virgin as she pretends to be. The guy she used to live with had my wife's cherry when she was sixteen."

"I just think you did the scene wrong," Carol said. "Being drunk and acting drunk don't look the same. Acting drunk looks more real."

"It was just an experiment. I thought it might work."

"I bet you it doesn't."

"Are you going to print this?"

"I don't see how I can fit it in."

"We're wrapping up next week."

"I thought I'd leave the day after tomorrow."

"Tomorrow's our day off," he said, "so I guess I won't be seeing you again. Too bad I'm married. You and I could have had fun." He hung up.

Carol had almost fallen asleep when the phone rang again. It was Atalanta, groggy from the sedative but still hysterical. She kept begging Carol not to write about what had happened and Carol kept promising her she wouldn't.

The next day there was a race and three horses piled up. A jockey was killed and they had to shoot two of the horses. Carol was horrified.

She went to her hotel room alone and tried to find some meaning in all of it: the men and the animals getting hurt and killed for the work they liked, the director tormenting the actress and both of them already killed inside. Had anybody ever asked the horses whether they liked their work? Maybe they didn't know the difference. She remembered the racing driver who had been hurt, and his friend who took it so calmly because, after all, they were in a game of death and the alternative was obscurity. The director tormented the actress because he was afraid his picture would not be a success, and the actress took it because she wanted to be a star. To them it was a life-and-death game, just as the horses and jockeys and racing drivers were really playing a life-and-death game. It just depended on the degree. It just depended on what was important to you.

She wished she could write about it in her article, but she knew it wasn't what the magazine wanted. They had told her to make it all glamorous and fun. They had even put a working title on the article: "Sexy Little Big Men."

She had told them they could use that title over her dead body. They had laughed and told her she wasn't the editor.

She got out her address book and put through a long distance call to Luciana in Milan. The maid was thoroughly confused by her bad Italian and finally put Bruno on the phone.

"It's Carol."

"Carol? Yes, Carol, ciao Carol, how are you?"

"I'm fine. I'm in England. I wrote to Luciana, did she get my letter?"

"I don't know," he said.

"How is she? How are you?"

"I am well."

"And Luciana? Is she there?"

"Luciana is in a clinic," he said. "You didn't know?"

"No, no. She hasn't written. What's wrong with her?"

"She had a nervous breakdown."

"My God! When did it happen?" What a stupid question—what difference did it make when it had happened?

"Six months ago. I don't know very much about it. We have been separated before it happened."

"I didn't know that either."

"Yes. If you want you can call her mother. But she is in Sicily. I don't know the number, Luciana took it with her things when we separated."

"Tell me the name of the clinic," Carol said. "Can I visit her?"

"She wouldn't know you. She doesn't want visitors."

"But why did it happen?" Carol said. *"Why?"*

"Why?"

"Yes, *why?* Luciana was never crazy."

"Luciana was always crazy," Bruno said calmly.

The next day on the plane to America the stewardess gave Carol the English newspapers. The story about the deaths of the jockey and the two horses was on the front page. All she could think about was Luciana. How could you ever tell who was going to hold out and who was going to fall apart? The psychology books would say it all started in the black spider's childhood, when her mother destroyed her ego by telling her she was ugly. But being rejected by a husband with a harelip couldn't have done her any good. She must have felt she was worthless. She must have always felt she was worthless. Those demented paintings which people were so eager to buy; to them it was just interesting art.

She could hear Luciana's voice: "You are not clever."

She could hear her own mother's voice: "Don't be *too* intelligent."

What was clever? What was intelligent? Luciana had been joy, a woman who enjoyed life. Carol felt very lonely.

9

"Come for din-din," Billy said. "I'll cook. I'm supposed to hear this afternoon if I have a job, and we can celebrate."

She was glad for Billy; he had been out of work now for so long his unemployment had run out and he had to accept handouts from his mother, who wanted him to leave evil New York and come home to live with her. Carol bought some flowers on the way and brought them to him.

"For your celebration."

"For my grave," Billy said. "I didn't get it."

"Oh, I'm so sorry."

"I can't understand it. They loved my résumé. The old fruit in Personnel kept cruising me. I thought I had it made."

"Did you camp?"

"I never camp."

"Billy—"

"That whole place is full of fags. Do you know how many fags they have working there, all pretending to be straight?"

"That's the point. They didn't want you to blow their cover, if you'll pardon the expression."

"Nobody would ever take me for gay."

"Billy, why don't you just buy a navy blue suit and a striped tie and try to look square?"

"I want people to accept me as I am."

"Then why do you act so crazy? You're not crazy—*that's* the act, being eccentric. You're bright, you're efficient, you work hard—"

Billy swept a long string of fake pearls off the top of the dresser and tossed them over his head. "Do you like my pearls?"

"No."

He bit one. "Funny . . . the Shah swore they were real."

"Can I help you with dinner?"

"No, but you can keep me company while I cook. I even bought some vodka. I thought we'd be celebrating. Now we can use it for the wake."

"You'll get something else," Carol said.

"I'd better. I'm going crazy here day after day." He took off the pearls and arranged them carefully around a bisque statue of a nude woman which was holding up a beaded lampshade. "Do you want to buy this lamp?"

"I don't need it."

"It cost fifty dollars. I'll sell it to you for twenty-five."

"I just don't need it."

"It's a horror, but you know, this sort of thing is going to come back. You'll be glad you have it."

"It doesn't go with my apartment."

"Twenty?"

"All right," Carol said. "But not with the pearls."

She sat on the kitchen ladder while he mixed the salad. He really wasn't a very good cook; the most elaborate thing he could make was meat loaf. He played old Marlene Dietrich records, and they drank the vodka while the meat loaf was baking.

"Did I ever show you my treasures?" Billy said. He went to the dresser and took out a tooled-leather jewel chest with a hinged top and velvet-lined drawers. From it he began removing cuff links, tie tacks, wrist watches, gold chain bracelets, rings. "This was from a producer," he said, holding up a ring. "And this was from a song writer." He held up a bracelet. "This was from a college professor, comparative literature." He held up a pair of cuff links set with diamonds. "They belonged to his father. This was from my first serious lover, our wedding ring. This watch and these cuff links were from a movie star, a sex symbol; I'd tell you his name but you'd die. This tie tack and the diamond studs someone left me in his will. Look, the tie tack is a peregrine falcon. This ring is a two-carat diamond, I had it appraised. He was married. His wife thought he was sneaking out to see another woman. She wasn't far wrong." He laughed maniacally.

"Nobody gives me jewelry," Carol said.

"I had everything," Billy said. "Everything. What's happened? Where has my life gone? It's all shit. Shit."

"Things will be better. You'll see."

He put each piece carefully back into the jewel box. "You know," he said sadly, "when I die, I don't even know who to leave them to."

"It's a little premature to worry about that," Carol said.

"You never know. I'd jump out the window but my hips would never fit." He laughed again. "Besides, it's only the second floor." He put the jewel box back into the dresser. "Come here, I want to show you my real treasures."

She followed him into the bathroom. He opened the medicine chest. Bottles and bottles of pills and capsules in neat rows. Most of them looked the same.

"There's my insurance," Billy said.

"Promise me you won't."

"I promise you I might."

"Nothing can be as bad as being dead," Carol said. "It sounds nice now, but you don't get a second chance. Suppose you were lying here dead and the phone was ringing with someone offering you the best job in the world."

"I'd tell them," Billy said, rolling his eyes and putting on his Bette Davis voice, "too bad. You should have known me when I was a star."

10

Carol ran into Peter Lugosi at a screening. "I read your piece," he said. "I didn't know you could write."

"Thank you."

"You were right about the drunk scene. It looked lousy. I had to cut it out of the picture."

She didn't say anything.

"That really was a good piece," he said. "From now on you can come on any picture I direct. As my guest."

Sure, she thought. As long as I don't write anything you disapprove of.

"I'll be in touch with you," she said.

11

She had lunch with Ellen to celebrate her promotion. Ellen had been transferred to another part of the agency and now had her own clients. Carol's agent never kept a secretary for long; either they cracked up from overwork or they got promoted. She hated it every time he got a new secretary. The new girl never knew her name and lied to her, saying he was busy, until she discovered Carol was one of the clients she was supposed to be nice to.

"I'm getting married," Ellen said.

"Well, for goodness' sake. Which one?"

"His name is Michael. You never met him. You'll like him. He's very sweet and bright and funny."

"I'd love to meet him."

"You might think he's kind of young."

"What is he, nineteen?"

"No, he's my age."

"What's wrong with that?"

"It just seems funny for either of us to be married. I don't feel like a grownup."

"Don't tell that to your clients."

"They're giving me a month off," Ellen said. "To get ready for the wedding. My parents want to have a big one."

"What do you have to do for a month?"

"Find an apartment. Decorate it. Pick out my china and silver and linens and stuff. Get a wedding dress. It's all so horrible. Luckily my parents are making out the guest list, so I don't have to bother with that. I want you to come. They're letting me have four friends of my own."

"That's sweet of them."

"Well, you know what weddings are," Ellen said. "It's just a way for the parents to pay back all their social obligations. I get the feeling if I sent a stand-in nobody would know the difference. The whole thing makes me sick. I wish we could elope."

"Why don't you?" Carol said.

"And break my parents' hearts?"

"You're going to keep working afterward, aren't you?"

"Of course. I could never be a housewife. I'd be too bored."

"What do you want for a wedding present?"

"One plate," Ellen said.

"*One* plate?"

"Wait till you see what they cost. You see, everybody in the family has to have the same dishes, so if any of us decides to have a dinner party for fifty people they'll all match."

"Where are you supposed to put these fifty people?"

"Nobody thought about that. I guess in the big house

in the suburbs I'm supposed to have when we're rich and have children."

"And to pick these dishes you already know about you have to take a month from your job?"

"It's what's done," Ellen said. "In my family you do what's done."

"Or otherwise you'll—"

"Break my parents' hearts," Ellen and Carol finished in unison. They both laughed.

"I don't know why I'm laughing," Ellen said. "I really feel like screaming."

12

The new secretary, Ginny, was a jolly girl who announced right away that she expected to be a full-fledged agent within a year. Carol hoped that meant she would work hard. The first thing Ginny did was give a Halloween party and invite all the clients she had ever met. Carol didn't want to go, but she was worried about Billy, who hadn't left his apartment for weeks, so she persuaded him to come with her.

He looked awful. She wondered if he'd been dipping into his pills. She picked him up at his apartment and paid for the cab to the party. He pretended not to notice and she knew he was embarrassed.

"When I get a job I'll make it all back to you," he said.

"I know you will."

Ginny lived in an East Side single girl apartment with the extra ice cubes in the bathtub so that when you went to get them you would be spared neither the view of her pink douche bag hanging from the shower head nor her transparent black bikini underpants drying on the shower rod. She was wearing a caftan, not because it was chic right then but because she was fat, and the pants on the shower rod, which were the stretch kind that looked tiny and fit anyone up to size twenty, gave promise of the wonders to come hidden under her tent. Carol wondered how many of the scruffy men sitting around the living room were or had been her lovers. She didn't see any clients, and realized she was probably the only one who was going to come. Ginny was wearing a resplendent blond synthetic fall, which didn't quite match the color of her hair.

"I didn't know this was a costume party," Billy said.

"Shh," Carol said.

There was some godawful rum punch Ginny had found the recipe for on her recent trip to Saint Thomas, and the usual gray dip with the broken potato chips sticking out of it. Girls were sitting on men's laps and being very vivacious. The only two pretty girls in the room were talking to each other, complaining how they couldn't find anyone they could stand to date. There were jack-o'-lanterns from the five-and-ten set around the room and a paper skeleton tacked to the wall over the studio bed. After what seemed like hours, one of the men went out and brought back pizza, and everyone fell on it as if they hadn't seen food for a week. Carol didn't get any, but she didn't care. She was sorry she had dragged Billy to this party, and sorry she had come herself. Everyone was too young. She hadn't been to a party like this in years, and she wondered if she'd ever thought they had been fun.

A man came over and sat next to her. "Is that your husband?" he asked, indicating Billy, who was sitting on the floor at her feet.

"No."

"Which one is your husband?"

"None of them." She didn't ask him which one if any was his wife because she didn't care.

"Are you divorced?"

"No. Why?"

"You look divorced."

"How does one look divorced?"

"Well, you're attractive, so I thought someone would have married you."

"I have been married several times," Carol said. "In the eyes of God." She immediately hated herself for still having to prove to idiots like him that men had loved her. That's what happened when you went through the time tunnel to your past. You forgot everything you had learned. No more parties like this, ever. She had to control herself. Other people had a right to be idiots, but she didn't. She could say that her life, the point at which she had arrived, was an accident, but she knew there were no such accidents. She had chosen to be a freak: a woman with no husband, no children, no cat, no dog, no goldfish, a woman with a nice apartment, a good job, enough money if she worked at it—and she always did—a woman who was attractive enough for people to ask her stupid questions, who found sex when she needed it and love from her friends. She was thirty-one. A woman like that was not supposed to be happy. She wasn't happy, but she wasn't nearly as unhappy as she had been when she was twenty imagining what it would be like now.

"Let's go to P.J.'s," she said to Billy.

"You're not leaving?" Ginny shrieked when she saw them in the hall by the door. "You just got here. Lots of people you know are coming. They promised."

"We have to meet some people," Carol said.

"Well, I'm awfully glad you came," Ginny said. "Really. And your friend." She smiled at Billy. "Are you a writer?"

"No," Billy said.

"What do you do?"

"I'm a bubble dancer."

"You're an actor?"

"No."

"Well, you look like you're in the arts."

"Happy Halloween," Billy said.

When they got out to the street, he said, "You don't really want to go to P.J.'s, do you?"

"I'm starving."

"I don't have any money."

"It's my treat. To make up for that awful party."

"I'm really depressed. I'd better go home."

"Have a hamburger first. Please. I'm depressed too."

"Why should you be depressed?" Billy said. "You have everything."

She had a hamburger but Billy wanted only coffee. She ordered pie with ice cream and then told him she was too full to eat it and handed it to him, but he didn't want it either. He was smoking too much. They walked back to his apartment and watched television for a few hours. When she went to the bathroom Carol looked into his medicine chest. The arsenal of pills looked fairly intact.

"I'm going home now to be mugged," she said. "If you get lonesome, call me."

"I will."

She kissed him good-bye. He waited at the door of his apartment till the self-service elevator came.

"If you see anybody cute in the elevator," Billy said, posing, "send him up."

13

Freddie called. "I've just come back from Moscow."

"Moscow!"

"It was fantastic. Listen, Carol, I have a story for us to do together, for *Life* magazine. I told them about you and they said okay."

"*Life* magazine!" Carol was excited. "Thanks, Freddie!"

"It's a dog's birthday party."

"You get to go to Moscow and I get to go to a dog's birthday party."

"You don't want to do it?"

"Of course I want to do it. Do you think it will conflict with the cat's bar mitzvah I'm doing for *Look?*"

He laughed. "Okay, it's tomorrow afternoon."

"What does one wear to a dog's birthday party?"

"A little diamond collar and a fur coat," Freddie said.

The party was in a high-rise apartment. Carol wondered if people really gave birthday parties for their dogs or if they were just having this one for publicity. There were men and women sitting around the living room, all looking self-conscious, all dressed up, each holding a small dog which was also dressed up; some of the dogs in clothes, some in bows and jeweled collars, all of them wearing colored toenail polish. Some of the dogs were dressed to match their owners' ensembles. There was a lace tablecloth on the table and a large birthday cake with candles on it and decorated with a small plastic figure of a dog.

Freddie was busy setting up lights. The hostess, a middle-aged woman in beige lace with orange hair piled up in an elaborate coiffeur, swooped down on Carol. "Come have a drink," she said. "Vodka?"

"That would be fine. Thanks."

"Do you have a dog?"

"No, I don't."

"But you love the little doggies, don't you? Of course you do, or you wouldn't be here."

"Oh yes, I love dogs."

"It's a shame you don't have one. I could get you a puppy if you're interested. Does your husband like dogs?"

"I'm not married."

She looked interested. "Oh? Neither am I. I like dogs much better than men, anyway; they're much better company. They don't talk back." She laughed. "Tonic?"

"Please." The woman poured almost an entire glassful of vodka. "That's too much," Carol said. "I have to work."

"Oh, it's only eighty proof."

When the woman turned her back Carol poured some of the vodka into the sink and added more tonic.

"The cake is made of meat," the woman said. "It's

my own recipe. The dogs love it. But it looks just like a regular birthday cake, doesn't it? I'm Bette DuVal. Bette with an *e,* DuVal with a capital *V.* Don't you write things down?"

"No. I remember."

"How intelligent you must be. Writers are so intelligent. I'm a designer myself. I have a new line of clothes coordinated for dogs and their mommies. I want you to meet the birthday boy. He's wearing one of my creations."

Bette led Carol into the living room and introduced her to another large woman who was wearing a sailor suit trimmed with sequins and holding a white poodle who was dressed in a matching sequin-trimmed sailor suit, complete with sailor hat which was secured under the dog's chin by a rubber band. The dog had a nervous tic. So did the woman. Or vice versa.

"This is Helen. And this is Sonny Boy."

Carol shook the dog's paw. He was wearing red nail polish. Freddie had started snapping pictures. Nobody was doing anything; they were sitting there stiffly, as if for a family portrait. Freddie pulled them around, put two of the dogs at the table and set champagne glasses in front of them, got one of the dogs to ride a tricycle the owner had brought. Carol asked people their names and occupations, what their dogs' special talents were, and if they often had occasions of this kind. She was very bored. The party was obviously a setup—publicity for Bette DuVal's line of clothes, and she hoped Freddie's pictures would be funny enough to get the story accepted anyway. Before she knew it she'd finished the glass of vodka. Bette DuVal swooped on her with a refill.

"Enjoy yourself," Bette said. "This is a party."

There was a little, bald old man shaking in the corner with a Chihuahua shaking on his lap, both of them featuring maroon velvet jackets. Doubtless another Bette DuVal creation. Carol drank her vodka. She was getting high and it was not so boring. Freddie made her hold a dog and took her picture for a souvenir. The dog was wearing sunglasses, and when she put him down he walked into a chair leg. Carol felt like calling the ASPCA to come and raid the place.

"Isn't this great?" Freddie whispered to her. "They're all so sick."

"Do they really take this seriously?"

"They do, they do." He put a new roll of film into one camera. "Where's DuVal's dog? He's supposed to play the piano."

Powderpuff was under the piano chewing a rawhide bone. He was a white poodle in a miniature tuxedo, and when Bette DuVal propped him on the piano chair on top of two telephone books, he put his paws on the keys and howled.

"He's singing!" everyone cried with glee. Freddie ran around taking pictures from all angles.

"Make Annie play 'Happy Birthday,' " someone said. They all applauded. One of the women, in a taffeta cocktail dress, rose and took Powderpuff's place at the piano.

"She's very talented," Bette DuVal said to Carol, putting another glass of vodka into her hand. "You have a treat." Then she put her arm around Carol's waist.

What Annie lacked in talent she made up for in noise. She pounded the keys, doing a ragtime version of "Happy Birthday," stomping the pedals. She was wearing spike heels, and there were dents in the linoleum where she had stamped. When she had finished "Happy Birthday" she went into more of her repertoire, and when she was finally finished everybody cheered. Carol looked at the dents in the floor. They were really there. Bette put her head on Carol's shoulder. "Wasn't that great?"

"Fantastic."

Bette gave her a little squeeze and let her go. "Now, the cake!"

The owners each set his or her own dog on a chair, paws on the table, and Freddie snapped pictures while Sonny Boy, with Helen's help, cut the cake. Most of the dogs ate, but two of them preferred to sniff each other.

"Maybe we will have a wedding," Freddie said.

"No," Helen said. "They're both girls."

Bette DuVal was back at Carol's side. "Is Freddie your boyfriend?" she whispered.

"No. My good friend."

"He's awfully cute."

"Yes, he is," Carol said. She looked at Freddie. Was he cute? She had never thought of him as attractive, but from his track record evidently a lot of other women did. She liked him, and he was sane, which was a relief.

He was so good at his work, she really admired him for it. Was he attractive? She was drunk, and she was not really sure. Maybe he was attractive, and he'd been right there all the time.

When the party was over, Freddie came back to Carol's apartment. Without giving it any thought she went to bed with him. It simply had never occurred to her before.

"I've always loved you," Freddie said.

She felt embarrassed, responsible. He was her friend; he shouldn't be in love with her. She believed him and she didn't want to think about it. She kissed him and didn't answer.

The phone rang. "What are you doing?" a woman's voice said.

"Who is this?"

"Bette DuVal."

"Oh. Hello."

"You were pretty drunk and I thought I'd call to see how you were."

"I'm fine," Carol said.

"I lost my bet," Bette DuVal said.

"What was your bet?"

"I bet Helen I could get you drunk and get you. But I didn't. But can I? Can I get you?"

"No," Carol said. "My photographer already did."

As it turned out, *Life* didn't use the piece. Freddie told Carol that they commissioned lots of things they never used. It wasn't something to get upset about. She and Freddie never went to bed together again, and neither of them ever mentioned that night. They remained friends. Freddie was clever and perceptive. Carol wondered sometimes afterward if she'd made a mistake in not trying to fall in love with him. She wondered if he had really loved her. They had their work in common, he was fun to be with, she would not be alone. She could have tried to give it a chance. But he wasn't the right one. There was a mean streak in him somewhere which she was wary of. But what was the use in trying to make up excuses for not falling in love with him? He just wasn't the right one.

14

The phone rang, waking Carol from a sound sleep. At first she could not recognize the voice, it was so blurred.

"I called . . . to say . . . I love you. Good-bye."

It was Billy, either full of pills or dead drunk.

"Billy? What did you take?"

"You're my good friend. My . . . only friend."

"Billy, what did you take?"

"My . . . insurance. Good-bye." He hung up.

Damn him. She put on the light, lit a cigarette, and then dialed his number. After several rings she heard the sound of the receiver being taken off the hook and laid down. Damn him. She dressed quickly and took a cab to his house.

After ringing his bell and pounding on the door she realized he either wasn't going to open it or couldn't. She went downstairs and woke the super.

"He's sick," she lied. "He has diabetes. You'd better let me in with the pass key so I can get his doctor."

The super let her in and came in with her to be sure she wasn't a burglar. The phone was off the hook and Billy was lying on the floor. He was breathing very shallowly and was a strange color. There was an empty bottle of sleeping pills on the floor near him, and his jewelry—his treasures—was scattered all around the room.

"Oh boy," the super said. "A burglar must have killed him."

"He's not dead."

"Maybe I'll call the police, " he said tentatively, obviously not wanting to get involved.

"Go back to bed. I'll take care of it."

The super was eyeing the jewelry with interest. He pushed a large ring with the tip of his shoe, not wanting to get fingerprints on it. "That's a diamond."

Carol picked up the empty pill bottle, looked at the doctor's name on the label, and then looked the doctor's number up in Billy's address book. The answering service answered.

"The doctor is not available," the disembodied voice said.

"You tell that pill pusher that one of his patients just tried to croak himself with his little goodies," Carol said, angry. She gave the voice Billy's name and number. Then she tried to pick him up, but he was too heavy.

"Help me."

The super took hold of Billy gingerly, as if he were going to be contaminated, and lifted him to his feet. "Crazy," he was muttering, "crazy."

"Walk him around while I make some coffee," Carol said. She made instant coffee, dropped an ice cube into it so it wouldn't burn Billy, and tried to get him to drink it. He was too far gone. She ran back to the kitchen and got a pitcher of cold water. She threw the water in Billy's face. He didn't react. She didn't know what else to do; her knowledge of how to cope with someone who'd tried to kill himself with sleeping pills was all garnered from doctor shows on television. The phone rang.

It was the doctor. He didn't sound at all upset. He said he would come over and to keep walking the patient around. Carol gathered up Billy's jewelry and put it back in the box. The super looked at her suspiciously.

"He was just playing with it," she said. "He does that sometimes."

"This house is full of crazy people," the super said. "We had a woman jump out the window once. Right in front of her husband. And this man, about four years ago, he threw his wife's dog out the window. Can you imagine? Why would someone want to do a thing like that?"

"I don't know."

"This other woman, she took up with a colored guy.

Her husband caught them. They had a fight and tore the whole place apart. They got evicted. So when she moved out, she painted the refrigerator black and took it right with her. The moving men just carried it out. Nobody noticed until it was gone. It cost two hundred and fifty dollars, the refrigerator. Huh."

"He looks terrible," Carol said.

"He's not walking, you know. I'm just dragging him."

"Please don't stop. The doctor said to do it."

"Good thing them faggots are light. Did you ever notice how skinny they always are? I know what goes on in this house."

"I guess you do."

"He's not bad for one of them," the super said. "He doesn't pick up people or give wild parties. We had one here once, he used to give parties and run down the halls in his underwear. We had this old lady, kind of senile, she came down to complain about it. But the funny thing was, she was in *her* underwear. They put her in an old age home. The fag they kicked out. I bet she just wanted to go to his party." He chuckled.

"I wish I knew how to make him throw up."

"Not on me he doesn't."

"God."

The doorbell rang and Carol let the doctor in. He was a dapper older man and she disliked him on sight. The doctor gave Billy a shot of something and he started to come around. He checked Billy's pulse a few times and stood up.

"He'll sleep normally now. Can you stay with him?"

"Yes. Let me show you something." She went into the bathroom and brought out two handfuls of bottles of sleeping pills. "They all have your name on them. And there are more. Don't you know better than that?"

The doctor looked at her with distaste. "I am not a policeman. If my patients squirrel away their pills, I can't spy on them. Some of those pills are so old they wouldn't do any good."

"I doubt that."

"Oh, you are a doctor?"

"No. Are you?" She tossed the pills into the doctor's bag. "Give them to somebody else."

"Have him telephone me tomorrow and tell me how he is," the doctor said, tight-lipped, and left.

"Huh," the super said.

Carol gave him ten dollars and he left. She locked the door. Billy was sleeping on the bed. Since the bed was the couch during the day, there was no place for her to sleep so she settled on a chair. She felt numb.

Billy woke up at two the next afternoon in rather good spirits. He wanted to know everything that had happened, and was pleased by the attention. But when she told him she had gotten rid of his pills he looked terrified.

"Those were mine!"

"So's your life. This is a free country. The next time you decide to kill yourself, don't bother to call me."

"You cared. You saved me."

"You get one chance. I'm warning you. I should have sent you to Bellevue, then they'd have given you a psychiatrist. I think you should go to somebody. Not that quack."

"I like that quack."

"I think you should go to a psychiatrist."

"I don't need a psychiatrist. I need a job."

"Then get a job. Be a waiter."

"I couldn't do that."

"It would get you out of the house."

"I have to work in my field. I can't go down; then I'd really kill myself."

"How about group?"

"Group what?"

"Group therapy. It's supposed to be cheap."

"I need group sex," Billy said in his Bette Davis voice. "What I need is love."

15

After that she called Billy every night to check on him, like a mother. He seemed normal and said he was starting to have a social life. Then he said he was going home to spend the weekend with his parents. It never occurred to her he was lying.

On Wednesday he called her from the hospital.

"I nearly died," he said, "but some friends saved me."

"Pills?"

"Yep. They said ten minutes more and I wouldn't have made it."

"You're sounding very pleased with yourself."

"You should see all the flowers I got," Billy said. "I'm surrounded by flowers. You're the only one who didn't send me any."

"I didn't know you were in the hospital."

"You know now. You can still send me some; I'm going to be here another two days. You can come visit me."

"Is it a mental hospital?"

"No, of course not. It's Lenox Hill."

"You must have pull."

"I have friends," Billy said.

"See? And you were complaining you didn't have any."

"It's a shame I had to nearly die to prove it, isn't it?" he said. "Are you going to send me flowers or not?"

"Not. I'm not going to encourage you."

"When I get out, maybe we can go some place. Would you go some place with me? My mother gave me money, we can go to Bermuda."

"All right."

"I forgive you for not sending me flowers," Billy said. "But I think you're cheap. I always knew you were cheap. I guess each of us has his little neurosis, don't we?"

When he got out of the hospital Carol went to his apartment to visit him. He had bruises on his face.

"Did somebody beat you up?"

"No, that's from the pills. When you take too many barbiturates, it breaks the blood vessels under the skin. You should see my body. I'm a mess. I don't think we should go to Bermuda, I think we should go to Florida. The weather's better there now. Key West. We could go to Key West."

"All right."

"I'll lie in the sun and become a bronze sex symbol."

"When do you want to go?"

"Next weekend. I have some things to do first."

The next afternoon Carol read in the newspaper that Billy had been found dead in his apartment of an overdose of sleeping pills. The reason it was in the paper was that there was jewelry strewn all over his apartment and at first it had been thought to be a crime of violence. But he had scrawled several notes, none of them to her.

She felt she had failed him. What could she have done? She felt guilty and sad. What a tragic waste. Billy hadn't killed himself, life had killed him.

It was hard to realize he was gone, but he was.

16

It was the mid-1960's, the Swinging Sixties as people liked to call them, and Carol thought people always thought their decade was wild or roaring or swinging and then looked back and said how dull it had been. Still, the sixties were better for her than the past had been, although she still didn't feel she fit in. There were discotheques, and she danced all night not really knowing the dances, copying other people, until one night she got carried away by the music and just did whatever she felt like doing—and realized that some other people were copying her because they thought *she* knew the newest dance. There were strange new clothes; she wore them. All the girls had false eyelashes. She did too. Lipstick was out, but she had never worn it. California had swinging condominiums for swinging singles where you could find love by the basement washing machine. New York had singles bars. She wouldn't be caught dead at a singles bar as a predator, but as an interviewer of course she went, armed for the first time with a tape recorder so people would know she was not there for the same reason they were.

She met Randolph at Maxwell's Plum. It was the best singles bar, and he was its best customer. He was resplendent in a camel-colored suede suit, with a handsome, innocuous face that girls found irresistible. Carol thought he had the face of a rabbit embryo. His customary place was in a niche by the door so he could see who was coming in, next to the phone and the cigarette machine so he could meet girls without having to buy them drinks. He also took walks around the room, plowing his way through the mob at the bar. He saw Carol. It was her tape recorder he noticed first. It was his suit she noticed first. They sat at a small table and she interviewed him, then she turned off the machine and he bought her a drink.

"I want you to know this is very unusual for me," he told her. "I never buy girls drinks."

"No?"

"I just take them home."

He was a dentist, an oral surgeon, he added, and had never been married. "I'm a catch," he told her. He wanted to make movies. His hobby was girls, but his movies would be important, sensitive, and he was serious about it.

A girl with a thin, nervous face came up to them. "Randolph! Listen, I have to go. Are you coming?"

"Sit down," he said.

"I only have the baby sitter till midnight. That gives us an hour. Are we going or what?"

"I'm being interviewed," he said. "This is Carol Prince. Do you want to be interviewed?"

The girl looked at Carol. "Oh boy," she said. "Some

people will try anything to meet a man." She looked at the two of them with disgust and went away.

"I didn't introduce her to you because I forgot her name," Randolph said.

"I wish I could have interviewed her. I loved that line about the baby sitter."

"A lot of these chicks are divorced and have a kid. Young marriages are breaking up. It makes me feel old. It also makes me feel vindicated. I tell myself I'd be paying alimony. It makes me feel better to think that when I have to get up in the morning and make my own breakfast."

"I'm sure that doesn't happen too often," Carol said.

"You're right. I don't know why it's the pigs who always want to clean your apartment in the morning; the beautiful ones just want to go home."

"They're no fools."

"Would you like another drink or would you like to have one at my place?"

"Here," Carol said, "if you let me pay for it."

"You want to pay for *my* drink?" he said incredulously.

"No, I want to pay for my drink."

"That's all right. I never met a girl like you before."

They got the next drink on the house because Randolph was such a good customer.

"We could go to your apartment," Randolph said. "Do you live alone?"

"Yes, I live alone, and no, we can't go to my apartment."

"What do you want?"

"Nothing."

"Amazing," he said. "Would you like to be my friend?"

"We could try that."

"I'd like that," he said. "I'd really like that. I never had a girl for a friend. I'd like to try that. Let's be friends."

"All right."

The last time Carol had become friends with someone by declaring they would be was in ninth grade. She and Randolph became friends. She knew he would be a much better friend than a boyfriend and she was glad to have him. Funny things were happening to her friends; they seemed to disappear from her life, from marriage or mortality, and Randolph seemed like a fixture trapped in time, someone who would never change. That was why he had the face of a rabbit embryo; nothing had ever happened to it.

Freddie had fallen in love with a girl and they were living together. Carol hardly ever saw him anymore. Ellen had been married to Michael in a gigantic bacchanal—doves flew out of the wedding cake—which Carol had attended, and true to her promise she was still working. Ellen was ambitious. She and Michael had decided not to have children or perhaps to have them much later if they changed their minds. After three years all their parents' friends started asking them embarrasing questions. "When are you two going to have your first?" Ellen would hang her head, look tragic, and say, "We can't." Then the pest would go away appalled at the tragedy she had unwittingly uncovered, and Ellen and Michael would laugh for ten minutes.

Bernice's husband was doing very well in his business and they had bought a large house in the suburbs. The children were all in public schools: "After all, we pay taxes," Bernice's husband said; and Bernice went to the country club in her sports car and took tennis lessons. She had a full-time maid who also cooked.

Bernice wanted more children; her husband said three was enough. It upset her. "When I was having babies," she told Carol, "I always felt important. Now I feel like the one thing I do best has been cut off. Hank and I still talk about the children all the time, but it's not the same."

Bernice had a Sunday brunch, and Carol brought Randolph. There were about twenty people there and they played charades. Several of the people thought Carol and Randolph were engaged, and several others asked them when they would be. Everybody was married. Randolph made a date with one of the married women and met her during the week in the city. Her son turned out to have chicken pox and somehow Randolph caught it.

Carol had had it as a child, so she went to visit Randolph with a jar of calf's-foot jelly to cheer him up. He was in bed, blotchy and miserable.

"Chicken pox!" he said. "That's what you get from a married woman. No more married women. Just single chicks. From them all you get is crabs."

But he seemed very pleased about his unusual affliction and she knew he would tell everybody.

At a party Carol rediscovered her college friend Princess Margaret Rose Tenenbaum, who it turned out had been in New York all this time, working, and being kept by a married man. They both agreed that neither of them had changed at all, although of course they had both changed a great deal. But they resumed their friendship as if the years between had never happened.

She knew another couple, Paul and Sally, and there were various people from her travels who popped up occasionally, but all in all, as the sixties went by, Carol found she was living a quieter life. She wanted it that way. She had a great deal of work and enjoyed having time to do it. She was tired of discotheques, and stopped going long before they went out of style. It seemed abnormal to go out on dates; she had been dating for twenty years. No one should have to date that long. Having friends was different. It was amazing how easy it was not to think about sex anymore. You just didn't think about it and it disappeared. (She had always been very disciplined when she set her mind to something.) Suddenly, picking up a man at a party and taking him home seemed dangerous. What kind of freaks picked up strangers? When she was younger it had seemed fun, but now when the men were her age it seemed strange. What was wrong with them that made them still live this way? They might well ask what was wrong with her, but she was the one who was running the risk of being killed by a maniac. She was lucky it had never happened. Twenty-year-olds seemed safer, but twenty-year-old boys did not attract her.

She was tired of having to prove she was having fun all the time to justify her existence, to whom? If you were still single you seemed to have to prove to the world that you were having more fun than anyone else. So this was the dreaded life of an old maid that she had been warned about. But it didn't seem so bad, it was natural, and she liked it. She was thirty-eight, and because she had time to spend on no one but herself, she knew she was lucky enough to look ten years younger. She felt that something was going to happen to her, something exciting, if not this year then next year. . . . She didn't know what it was, but she felt it.

Approximately seventeen years after Carol had burned her girdles in the kitchen of her mother's apartment in private, some young women burned their bras in public in the streets of New York City. People were talking about Women's Lib. Carol was glad about Women's Lib, but she didn't see any reason to join in. She hadn't been able to wait for them, she had liberated herself long ago, in her work, in her life, in her head. Now people stopped asking her why she had never married. She was no longer a freak, she was a heroine. But to herself she was no heroine, she still had questions. She had never done any of the things she had done for a cause, she had simply drifted along trying to be true to her own needs. There were still so many things she had not done. She felt as if her self-imposed semihermit's existence was a chrysalis. Something was going to happen to her, she was going to burst out. . . . When it was time. . . .

17

On a winter Sunday morning she was going to a brunch with Henri, a friend from Paris whom she had met while doing a story on French bachelors. He was one of those friends from out-of-town, the sort you would never see if you both lived in the same place, but whom you felt obligated to see when he appeared, and who felt obligated to see you when you appeared; the etiquette of loneliness in a strange city. She really would have preferred to spend the day alone.

She was trying to decide how much makeup to bother with when the phone rang. It was Randolph.

"Is this Helen Gurley Brown?"

"No, fink." But when Randolph was into one of his routines, no one could stop him.

"Miss Brown," he went on in a fake falsetto, "I think you should get Carol Prince to write for your magazine because she is my favorite writer and I just loved the piece she did on the sex life of Lassie the Wonder Dog."

"I can't talk now, I have a wet eyelash in my hand," Carol lied.

"You're going out?" He was back to his own voice in a flash.

"I'm going to a party."

"Why didn't you invite me?"

"Because someone invited me."

"Is he there now?"

"No."

"Are you after him?"

"No."

"Then why can't you take me too? I'm all alone and I'm bored."

"What happened to the girl you were with last night?"

"She had to go to church this morning."

"To confess the dirty things you made her do."

"I wouldn't," he said, pleased. "Take me to the party. I need to meet someone. I want to fall in love."

"You say that every day."

"I never give up hoping."

It occurred to Carol that she kept up with Randolph because he bored her; he kept reminding her how rotten it was outside and made her glad she was not there. He was her age, and he still acted like a kid. She knew there were a lot of people like him; the men were known as Desirable Bachelors.

"Well, be here in half an hour and don't be late," she said. "If you're late we'll leave without you. And do not dress like a bum."

"I can't be there in half an hour if you keep me talking on the phone," he said, and hung up.

She was ready when Henri rang the bell. She was always ready on time when men came to her apartment, a carry-over from her naïve belief in the fifties when she first got her own apartment that if a man saw a girl alone in her underwear he would be overcome with lust and rape her on the spot. It amused her now to think that there were so many funny little habits one kept long after the reason for them was gone.

Henri was wearing a black suit with a vest, and a sheepskin-lined overcoat. His hair was tousled and his face was flushed from walking through the park, the innocent tourist, and he looked healthier than usual but still like a weasel. He too, like Randolph, was a Desirable Bachelor, French style.

She hung his coat in the closet and gave him some wine. He looked around the apartment to see if she had changed anything, and then he looked at her and said, "You look well, Carol. You look rested."

"I've been getting a lot of rest."

"Are you working?"

"I'm doing a piece on tits. It's a research piece."

"Tits?"

"*Gorge.*"

He smiled. "Do they actually read that rubbish in the United States?"

"You'd be surprised. Actually, it's about plastic surgery to make you bigger if you're small and smaller if you're too big. But I'm sneaking in my own opinion that the whole thing is ridiculous and people worry about it too much. Being flat chested never hurt Audrey Hepburn. And what are you doing?"

"The bank is the same. A bank. I've been promoted to vice-president."

"Good for you."

"Are you in love with anyone?"

"No," Carol said. "You?"

"I'm living with a girl. You know I can't fall in love with anyone, but she loves me, so I let her live with me."

"Touching."

"You're like me, Carol. You know there's no love. It's a childish lie." One of Henri's favorite words was childish, in reference to anything except himself.

"There's a guy coming with us, if you don't mind," she said. She got up and refilled the wine glasses. Henri covered his when she had poured about three drops into it.

"Not in the morning. This guy is your lover?"

"No, my son."

"Son?"

"He thinks he's my son although we're the same age. He says I'm very maternal."

"You're not maternal, Carol. You'll never get married, just as I never will. And you won't have children."

"The thing about you, Henri, is you're always so cheerful."

"But you are childish. You still believe in these things."

"I didn't say I believed in them. I just don't want not to believe in them anymore."

She was surprised she had said that. But what she had meant was that she never wanted to have to make a permanent decision for the rest of her life, never to have to say, It's over, nothing will change now. When you had decided nothing would ever change, then you were dead.

She was relieved when Randolph arrived. He had on a Cardin suit from Barney's and a six-inch-wide tie with a triple thick knot tied so high and tight that his head looked like one of those corks with a face on it about to pop out of its bottle. Rabbit Embryo Liqueur. A fine addition to Blue Nun and Black Cat in the Cellar.

"You are a writer too?" Henri said.

"He's a dentist."

"I used to be a dentist. I'm a filmmaker now."

Henri looked interested. "What have you done?"

"I've written six scripts. I'm trying to raise the money. I have a few studios bidding on two of them." She let him go on embellishing the lie about the studios for a while because she wanted Henri to think she had at least inflicted someone interesting on him, but then she got embarrassed when Randolph started dropping the names of his future fantasy stars, and she suggested they go.

The brunch was in an apartment on Fifth Avenue, high up, with a view of people ice-skating in the park. It was very pretty. There was a maid to take the coats, and perfectly mixed Bullshots and Bloody Marys. She was introduced to people and immediately forgot their names. Henri was talking to the people who had invited him, and Randolph had found a very young girl to take into the corner and impress. Carol looked out the window at the people ice-skating. She should take up ice-skating. All that fresh air. It was a shame she was so hopelessly unathletic.

Randolph came up to her. "You should talk to somebody," he said.

"I will."

"Would you like a drink?"

"Yes, please."

"Don't get drunk," he said. He went away and came back with three drinks, gave her one, and went away with the other two. Carol walked into another room.

People had begun to eat eggs benedict and quiche lorraine from a buffet, but she didn't bother because she wasn't hungry. Henri was standing up in a corner eating messily and jabbering to two other men in French. His face lit up when he saw her.

"Ah! There you are." He waved her over with his fork and they began talking French again. "You understand," he said to her once, and she nodded, although she didn't.

She was bored, and sorry she had come. After a while she drifted away from them without their noticing and stood on the periphery of a group of large bodies, men. The group seemed to open and she moved within it. She had evidently been introduced to most of them because they seemed to know her.

"This is Matthew Fitzgerald," one of the men said.

She and Matthew Fitzgerald started to nod hello, and then they both said in unison: "We've met."

She recognized him right away even though it must have been at least five years and he looked better because his hair was longer. She was surprised he remembered her. They went away from the others and sat down.

"Do you remember," he said, "we met at a party."

"Yes."

"You were drunk and you had on a yellow dress."

"I'm sure I was. But I don't have a yellow dress."

"You did."

She tried to remember. "Were you drunk too?"

"Of course," he said. "Who were you with?"

"I don't remember. Do you?"

"No. I took you out the next day, do you remember that?"

She couldn't and it was a little frightening. You met too many people through the years, and they meant so little. But she remembered him. Now she remembered distinctly the first moment she had seen him, that she had wanted to know him, and she felt the same way now, but she didn't recall ever going out with him, and that frightened her: had she gone to bed with him? She couldn't remember, and she hoped she had not, because that was not something you would want to forget.

"You didn't take me out," she said.

He pretended to look hurt, but he wasn't. "I called you the next day and came to your apartment for a drink—two drinks—and then I went away because I had an appointment."

"Did we do anything?"

"No. Don't you remember that either?"

And then she did remember.

He had been standing with people, just as he had this time, and someone had told her not only his name but who he was, what he owned, assuming she would be impressed by how important and rich he was. She recognized the name of the company, and the person who had introduced them said that Matthew Fitzgerald was president of that company, a bit of crassness that passes for social grace at New York cocktail parties. He had been standing very still at the center of that group, with space around him, and his physical presence seemed to jump out at her. He wasn't tall but he was powerful looking, with thick fair hair that had turned mostly gray, and he had the look and bearing of a former street fighter. The confidence of a street fighter who had always won, the aware, moving eyes of an intelligent street fighter who knows it is never over.

She remembered following him discreetly around the party, trying to think of something to say to him, finding him very easy to follow. She supposed they had spoken, because they had ended up with a small group of very drunk people at a discotheque. She had slipped him her telephone number, unasked, and the next day he had called and come to her apartment for a drink. He was married, so she had assumed it would be a drink and bed. But he had sat in the armchair and told her pleasant stories about his wild children and then he had gone away.

He had given her his telephone numbers and addresses in California and London, in case she ever went there, and she had been to both places but never called him. She had written his phone numbers in her almost real alligator address book and never called. She had spent months in London and California, once only two blocks away from where he lived, but she had never called.

It had been an instinct. Not an instinct which said he had forgotten her; she knew he would invite her immediately for dinner with his wife and friends—so perhaps that was why she had not called. It had not been the right time for him, she had sensed their lives would not fit. No, that was an afterthought; it was what she was thinking now. At the time she had simply forgotten him.

"I remember now," she said. "You gave me your phone number."

"You never called."

"Why did you come up for a drink anyway?" she asked.

"I thought you were one of those strange, nervous New York girls. I thought you might need someone to talk to. I was curious. I wanted to help you."

Was that how I seemed? How odd. "When a married man comes up to a single girl's apartment, he makes a pass at her. You didn't. Was I too nervous?"

"No. I knew you would knock me off and forget about me. I didn't want it to be like that."

"You were right," Carol said. "I would have knocked you off. I'm glad you didn't."

They went to the bar and had a couple of drinks. She felt comfortable with him and liked his calm. If anyone else had told her she had once been strange and nervous and needed help, she would have been antagonistic, looking for subterfuge. But this man didn't want anything from her, he was just making an observation of how she had seemed to him, and perhaps it was possible he was right.

She saw Randolph looking at her and Matthew Fitzgerald, and then leave the girl to come sidling up to them. The only two things in the world Randolph cared about were sex and money. The order of importance was interchangeable. He claimed money came first because it sounded more dignified. Evidently today it did. He put out his hand and introduced himself, wearing that unctuous innocent look on his face which tried to say he was only twelve years old, and which meant he was up to something.

"What do you think about the future of the motion picture business?" Randolph said.

"It stinks," said Matthew.

"I agree. You're very perceptive. I'm sure you know about all sorts of things that have nothing to do with your business. It's the only way to get anywhere in this world, and I can see you must know about everything or you wouldn't have gotten where you have. No, I'll just have a Coke, please. I happen to have a theory about the motion picture business, which I'd like to ask your opinion about. Could we sit down?"

"All right," Matthew said pleasantly.

They sat on a sofa with their drinks and Randolph's untouched Coke. Carol took out a cigarette and Randolph whipped out a book of matches and lit it, something he never did when they were alone.

"My theory about the motion picture business," Randolph went on, "and I know Carol agrees because I've discussed it with her—I believe the future is in the backing of private industry. That way the young film-maker is not under the control of those fossils who run the studios, and private industry can diversify and make profits which are far greater in the long run than anything it can make right now in this soft economy."

"It's possible," Matthew said.

"I used to be an oral surgeon, but I gave it up because I didn't feel it was where it's at right now. I want to be *now*. Carol is now. I can see you're now. It has nothing to do with age." He smiled winningly, meaning Matthew Fitzgerald's age, not his, since Matthew Fitzgerald was somewhere in his mid-forties and Randolph was obviously only twelve. "I used to make a hundred thousand dollars a year. I drove a Cadillac. But I gave it up. I felt constricted. I care about money just as much as the next person, and I feel there's just as much money to be made in the motion picture business doing it my way as there is spending my life putting caps on rich bitches who don't need them."

"If we're going to talk I need another drink," Matthew said.

They went back to the bar. Randolph rushed ahead of them and got the drinks. Carol took out a cigarette.

"I'm not going to light your cigarette," Matthew said. "You smoke too much. Light your own cigarette."

She did.

"You smoke too much," Randolph said. "I agree with you, sir. I gave it up. I couldn't breathe. Now I only smoke pot. Occasionally, of course." He looked for a reaction, but there was none. "I've written six beautiful now scripts, which Carol has read. She likes them. What I'd like to ask you, sir, if you have the time, is to read one or two of them and tell me what you think. They could be brought in very cheaply, under a million dollars in color. That's the magic figure: *under a mil-*

lion dollars. You use sixteen millimeter Jap blow and a non union crew. I'd want a star, of course, but I'd give him a piece of the picture instead of money."

"I don't know anything about the motion picture business," Matthew said.

"It doesn't matter. I do. I'd just like your opinion, if you could spare the time. I'd appreciate it very much."

"Send them to my office," Matthew said. He took out a small white card, looked at it, put it back, and chose another one. "This is my New York office." He gave the card to Randolph.

"Could you have dinner with Carol and me tonight?" Randolph said. "I know a wonderful place I bet you've never been. I know the owner. He's a millionaire hippie."

"All right," Matthew said pleasantly, but he was looking at Carol.

It was ridiculous, really, using such a transparent excuse to keep being with Matthew Fitzgerald; she felt like a shill. Ordinarily she could say, Buzz off, Randolph, I want to be with this man alone. But Matthew looked as if he wasn't fooled and didn't care. You didn't push this man around, he went at his own pace and did what he pleased. She decided to go with it and wait to see what happened. She hoped that Randolph would have the decency at least to try to split the check, but she doubted it.

18

Randolph called Carol the morning after they had dinner with Matthew Fitzgerald. "I sent him two scripts by messenger," he said. "I thought that would be enough. 'Highway' and 'Beverly.' I thought that was a good choice. When do you think I'll hear from him?"

"I don't know."

"Do you think those were the right ones to send him?"

"Fine," she said. They weren't any worse than the rest of Randolph's scripts.

"He certainly got drunk last night," Randolph said. "I think he's an alcoholic. He's very interesting though. Even when he's drunk."

"You think everybody is an alcoholic."

"My father was an alcoholic. I know all the symptoms."

"We all have our hobbies. You, for example, Randolph, are going to die someday of terminal clap."

"I never had clap. Never. I got syphilis once when I was interning and they gave me a welfare patient. I was extracting his tooth and the scalpel slipped. He had syph and I cut myself and had to have shots. That was why I gave up charity work. But I never got any disease from sex."

"Except chicken pox," she said and hung up on him.

He called right back. "We were disconnected. Do you think I should call him tomorrow or wait until the end of the week?"

"Who?"

"Old Matthew McBooze."

"Why don't you wait until he calls you?" she said. "I'm hanging up now. Good-bye."

Matthew Fitzgerald called her the following Sunday. "I've been in London," he said. "Your friend left three messages at my office while I was away. Tell him I haven't had a chance to read his scripts yet."

"Okay."

"Well—" he said.

"What are you doing?"

"Nothing."

"Do you want to come over for a drink?" Carol said.

"Fine. What time?"

"Four, five, six. Whatever's good for you."

"Four," he said.

She gave him her address again. It was two o'clock and she decided she would have enough time to wash her hair, even though she had washed it two days before.

When Carol opened the door he just stood there as if she wasn't going to ask him in. He looked different: formal, stern, wearing a black overcoat with a velvet collar. She didn't go out with anyone who wore a black coat with a velvet collar, and never had. She hung the coat in the closet and poured two drinks. He sat in the armchair and she sat on the couch.

"Your apartment looks different."

"It's redecorated."

"Blue is my favorite color," he said.

Then he made fingerprints on his glass and sat there not saying anything. She thought he was shy, so she jabbered on like a hostess about pleasant inconsequential things. He was hard to talk to, but he seemed interested, even grateful. She noticed his hands were shaking and wondered if it was true that he was an alcoholic.

He had two more drinks and then he was easier to talk to. It didn't seem strange that a man who was so powerful, who knew so many important people, who obviously had to speak to people to get what he wanted, should be so shy with her. She had met people like that. She thought he must be lonely being here alone, with his wife and children across the country. He had to be lonely if he had called on a Sunday afternoon when obviously people must have called him to invite him to brunches and cocktail parties and dinners. Maybe he just wanted to be with a girl.

She told him things about her family and her work. She did not say anything about her men. She left out anything that could possibly have been construed as neurotic or make her "one of those nervous New York girls." He was too sharp; she had to be careful. She couldn't imagine how he could be interested in these dull things, but she kept on talking, in a light, rather self-mocking sort of way, as if of course they both knew that none of these things really mattered because they were in the past, but still they were sweet.

"My childhood was comfortable and boring," she said. "I am an only child, as were most of my friends born during the Depression, but my parents scraped up enough money to send me to private schools. Both of them have college degrees. Of my class in college, about one-third became teachers or professors, all but one—me—got married, one died of cancer, one in an auto accident, and one was killed searching for Inca ruins. The average number of children per family is five. One girl has thirteen, twelve of them are boys, and the last six were born at home. Less than half of my classmates are divorced, and all the ones who were divorced but two have remarried. The girls who left school to get married and have children all went back to get their degrees when their children were old enough to take care of themselves. Several of them even have Master's and Doctor's degrees. The ones who bother to write into the Alumni Journal mention their husbands and children first, and then in passing mention that they are working at something extraordinary themselves. I don't keep up with any of them anymore."

He laughed. "I can see why not."

Much of Carol's social experience had been the sharp give-and-take that passes for conversation between men and women when there is sexual tension underneath, but with Matthew Fitzgerald she didn't feel any sexual tension; they weren't after each other. She was just a hostess and he was just a guest. Get the fresh ice cubes when his melted, fill the glass when it was empty, replace the glass with a clean one when there were too many fingerprints on it, offer him crackers and cheese which he refused, dump the ashtray when it got too full of her cigarette butts so it would not offend him as a nonsmoker—a hostess. He kept putting his glass down in a clean ashtray (her apartment featured a great many hotel ashtrays) even though the table had a glass top. His hands had stopped shaking after the third drink. That was one of Randolph's sure signs of an alcoholic; but if Matthew Fitzgerald was an alcoholic, why hadn't he started drinking at home?

"When I was a kid," he said, "we never had a book in the house. My parents are illiterate. They quit school in the sixth grade to go to work. But they always felt an education was the most important thing a person could have."

"Did you go to college?"

"Of course. I have three degrees."

"Scholarship?"

"I worked. My father threw me out of the house when I was sixteen because I was a Communist."

"Were you?"

"I suppose so, for those days."

"Do you still see him?"

"Oh sure. We're friends now. When you grow up you have to think your parents are funny. You can't keep on fighting with them."

"I wish I felt that way," she said.

"You should. You're an adult, why should you fight

with them? If you don't get along with them when they're alive, then when they die you have too much guilt."

"But they don't think I'm an adult. They want me to get married so I can have a legal guardian."

He smiled. "That's natural for parents."

"Will you want your daughter to get married?"

"I'll want her to do whatever makes her happy."

"Well, then."

"Of course, she's only twelve. I don't know what I'll think when she grows up."

The phone rang and she answered it in the bedroom. It was Randolph. "Do you think I should call Old McBooze on Monday when he gets back from London? Do you think I would be bothering him on his first day back?"

"Yeah, do that."

Randolph began doing a bad imitation of a drunk. Whenever he sensed he was going to be rejected he started putting the person down so he wouldn't be hurt. Today Carol found it very annoying.

"I can't talk to you now," she said. "My parents are here."

"Oh. Good luck." He laughed and hung up.

She went back to the living room. "Am I keeping you from anything?" Matthew Fitzgerald said.

"No, no, sit down."

"Do you have a date for dinner?"

"No."

"I have a tentative date, but I can call him and cancel it if you'll have dinner with me."

"Won't he mind?"

"No. It was just tentative."

"That thing on the floor that looks like a phallic symbol is the phone. Unless you'd rather use the one in the bedroom."

The one in the bedroom was for privacy and lies. That was the one he chose. She was surprised and flattered that he wanted to have dinner with her. He seemed like someone who always had a great many important things to do. But he probably had dinner every night with men, talking about business. Why shouldn't he want the company of a woman for a change?

19

During the next several months Carol saw Matthew Fitzgerald about once a week. He never asked her out; he just phoned, hemmed and hawed, and she asked him over for a drink. He would sit in the chair or stand looking out the window, his hands would shake, he would not talk until he had finished three drinks. She learned that of his class in high school twelve people had gone to prison, three had died in the electric chair, and two had become millionaires. One of the millionaires was him. His mother went to Mass twice a day even though the service was in Latin and she didn't understand a word of it. When they changed the service to English she didn't enjoy it more, she just liked the idea of going. His father did not go to church. Neither did Matthew, although his wife took the children. His wife, he said, was beautiful and brilliant and read a lot. He seemed to love her. Sometimes she overslept and the children went to church alone. Their house was furnished with antiques and had a swimming pool. He didn't seem to care about any of these things, the religion or the possessions; it was just something people did who had been very poor and were now very rich: they did the right thing.

He bought things: cars, clothes, shoes, gadgets, paintings, sculpture, houses. He had a complete wardrobe in every country and city where he kept a hotel suite or a house or an apartment, so he never had to take a suitcase. But his suits always looked as if he had slept in them, and he always had a hole in his monogrammed shirt or at least one of the buttons was missing. He had stains on his ties. He never seemed to notice.

He went to London and Paris and Madrid and California the way other people went to the country for the weekend. He had an air travel card. He slept on planes and never watched the movie. He got up at six o'clock every morning and was at the office before eight. He never had a hangover. He drank twenty cups of black coffee every day and never took uppers, although he took every other kind of pill imaginable for every possible, imaginable ailment. He said his doctor was a hypochondriac, and seemed to like the idea. She supposed the expensive hypochondriac doctor was another of the right things to have when you had been very poor and had become very rich. He said he had never been to a doctor or a dentist until he was twenty-one years old and could afford it.

What he learned about her, she didn't know. Most of it must have been by instinct, since she was most circumspect. Her past was her own. He knew executives, bartenders, movie stars, call girls, politicians, gangsters, artists, writers, bankers, secretaries, millionaires, bums, people who had been married four times, homosexuals, piano players, headwaiters, singers, old men who had given him jobs when he was young and whom he now hired, his wife's socialite friends, and Carol. But he said he had no friends. She knew what he meant.

He read Randolph's scripts and sent them back, saying he was not in a position to diversify his investments at the present time. Randolph asked him if he would find someone else who would. He said he would try.

She still thought of him by his whole name: Matthew Fitzgerald. She could not think of him as Matthew, and never as Matt. She never called him anything. She called him hello. She didn't remember him ever calling her anything either. When he telephoned he always said, "This is Matthew Fitzgerald," as if she knew five other Matthews or had forgotten him.

He never even touched her. He always took her home after dinner and sometimes came up for a drink afterward, but never kissed her good-night. One night they were standing on the street waiting for a taxi, it was cold, and he put his hand on her shoulder, very lightly and tentatively. It was more a gesture of protection than anything else; a man putting his hand on a girl's shoulder because it was a dark street in winter. His hand was shaking and he took it off her shoulder in a second. She told him he should wear gloves and he said he had lost them.

She liked that he did not touch her. Although she felt very safe and secure with him he frightened her. She told herself she could not go to bed with a man who wore a black coat with a velvet collar and had unreadable eyes. But the truth was he was there now, a part of her life, and she knew him. She didn't want anything to spoil it.

At the end of winter Carol went to Spain for two weeks to do a piece on a very successful expatriate American novelist. She loved the weather and the food and the heavy shutters on her hotel room windows, but she was sick the entire time. She had chronic stomach trouble: it felt like a squirrel on a treadmill was working away in her insides. It was colitis, and there were other unpleasant effects. She knew it wasn't the water or the time change, because she was always careful of her health, and besides, she had been sick in New York many times. It seemed as if she'd had Her Trouble forever, although she could remember years when she was perfectly well.

Everybody she knew had stomach trouble, except

Randolph, who had definite head trouble. Ellen had an ulcer. Princess Margaret Rose Tenenbaum, who had been going with her married man for twelve years, had colitis. Bernice was always constipated. They had all discussed it and decided it was the result of living in or near New York. Princess Margaret Rose Tenenbaum, however, said she got colitis from her married man.

Except for being sick, Carol found the work very easy in Spain because the novelist loved to talk about himself and gave her more material than she needed. The last night she was there he invited her to do a three with him and his girl friend. He said it was his girl friend's idea. Carol declined. He smiled understandingly, but his eyes turned into two little bits of gray stone.

When she got back to New York she wrote her usual charming, homey piece, about the beloved married novelist with the advanced sexual tastes and the mean eyes of a snake, leaving that part out of course. She concentrated on all the intellectual things he had told her, which now seemed like pretentious lies. She told of his juvenile pranks, which she described as human and boyishly sweet. (She wondered what was going to happen to his girl friend when he ditched her, but she supposed she could live on her jewelry until she found someone else. It might be nice to be kept, and travel around the world, if you could find someone nice. It must be interesting to be a girl who never worked on anything but her hair and her body and her complexion. Maybe she could write a piece on that kind of girl.)

It took her only three days to write the article, but she was sicker than ever: the squirrel in her stomach was working his treadmill double time. The editor she was dealing with on the magazine said it was too long and too kind and he wanted revisions. He said he wanted some tantalizing scandal. For the first time Carol told him to do the changes himself and she didn't care what he did. The editor was not displeased because he liked being creative. They paid Carol a thousand dollars, her agent got ten percent for doing nothing, and she put the rest of it in the bank to pay her bills. It occurred to her that the novelist's girl friend would have been envious; it must be hard for her to scrape up a thousand dollars in her line of work. But everybody had to pay his dues.

Carol could see the beginnings of spring outside her window, although it was still cold. She hated spring. Couples walked in Central Park holding hands on Sunday afternoons. Girls like she used to be gathered at the Bethesda Fountain to pick up men. Too much paper flew in the wind, dogs fouled the sidewalks, and she was tired of the park. So on Sunday afternoon she stayed home and washed her hair, and at three o'clock Matthew Fitzgerald phoned. She realized she had expected him to.

20

"I have to go to a cocktail party," he said. "Could you meet me for dinner?"

"Sure," she said.

"Where do you want to go?"

"I don't care."

"Then let's go to that place near you where we always go. I think of that as our place."

It was the first personal thing he had ever said and Carol didn't know if he was kidding or not. They arranged to meet at seven.

He was forty-five minutes late. She knew by then he would be drunk, but she hadn't known how drunk. She had seen him drink more than anyone she had ever known and hardly show it, but that evening he was really drunk, and something told her he had done it on purpose. "You're late and you're drunk," she said.

"I know." He ordered two drinks at once and she had the feeling it was going to be a bad evening. "You must be hungry," he said. "Let's order."

He ordered what she did, obviously not caring what he had, and then he pushed the food around on his plate and didn't eat it. He ordered two more drinks. Carol didn't know what was going on. There were strange vibrations. She was embarrassed because it was a small, very brightly lit restaurant and he was obviously drunk, spilling things, and she didn't want anyone to look at them. She felt like a prude, and also like his mother. Maternal, as Randolph would say.

Then Matthew Fitzgerald turned to her and said, his voice very blurry, like the caricature of a drunk, "I like you."

She smiled. She was glad.

"I like you very much," he said. "You're intelligent and talented and beautiful. You're a great dame. You're one of the greatest dames I've ever known in my life."

All she could think of was that nobody had said "dame" since the forties.

"I like you *very* much," he said.

Then she knew what was coming next, and although she wanted him to say it and it somehow did not surprise her, she also very badly did not want him to say it.

"I love you," he said.

That was why he had gotten drunk: because he wanted to tell her. Matthew Fitzgerald had never gotten drunk accidentally in his life.

"I love you," he said again. "I'm in love with you."

"Don't talk so loud," Carol said. "People are listening."

He tried to lower his voice. People really weren't listening, but she was afraid they were. "I just wanted to tell you," he said. He leaned over and put his arm around her.

"Not in a public place," she said.

He laughed. But then in a minute he was all over her again. "Not in a public place," she said.

"Not in a public place," he imitated, and he sounded like Donald Duck. They both laughed. "That's another one of the things I like about you," he said.

He was in love with her. It seemed inevitable. He was in love with her so now she would go to bed with him, and then she would get to know him too well, he would think he owned her, she would know all his faults and grow to hate him. It was too much of a bond, it was too close. The best part was always the beginning. She liked him so much she could not let him spoil it. She would not go to bed with him. Never.

"I want a stinger on the rocks," Carol said. "With a straw."

She had three stingers on the rocks with a straw. Then they were in a cab and she said, "Let's go to your place."

She knew perfectly well why she had drunk the three stingers.

The thing she noticed about being in bed with him that was different was the kissing: the fierce, desperate kissing, and the holding, like the desperate kissing and clutching of two people whose skins had been starved for love for years. He was not like anyone she had ever known, but neither was she.

When she woke up it was some ungodly early hour in the morning, and he was sitting on the edge of the bed, dressed in a dark suit and tie, looking at her with the sad and tender look of people at airports and railroad stations. He looked at her that way for a long time and then he kissed her good-bye and said, "You sleep."

He left and she went to sleep.

It was noon when she got up and she didn't know where she was. She couldn't find all her clothes for a long time. She dressed and went into his bathroom where she brushed her teeth with the toothbrush she still carried in her purse from force of habit, and his toothpaste, which she was pleased to discover was her brand. She washed off her makeup, noticing that she looked like a raccoon. She brushed her hair with his brush, picked out her hairs and threw them into the wastebasket. Then she looked at the apartment.

It was one of the strangest apartments she had ever seen because it looked as if no one lived there. Everything was spartan and immaculately clean. There was nothing personal. It looked like a place where he slept and made phone calls. There was one cup and saucer, neatly washed and turned upside down on the drainboard to dry, one plate, several spoons and knives but no forks, a jar of instant coffee and a tin of imported cookies. In the refrigerator under the sink was some skimmed milk, some diet jam, a loaf of diet bread, and four jars of mustard. There was a small tape machine on the sideboard, but no television set and no radio. Then she remembered seeing a tiny portable radio hanging on a hook over the bathroom sink, which had apparently been one of two hooks that held a glass shelf, long since broken and thrown away and never replaced.

The bookcase held quite a few books without dust jackets and at least twenty bottles of various pills.

She inspected his tapes. She was surprised that most of them were the best rock albums, all of which she had. There were also several dreadfully corny albums of background music, the kind that would belong to a man who said "dame."

She thought of making coffee but she wanted to get out of there. She lit a cigarette and left.

When she got into the hall she couldn't find the door. There were several doors, but they were either to other people's apartments or to the back stairs. She remembered coming up in an elevator but she couldn't find it. She did find a window, and looking out of it realized he was high up. She didn't want to walk down that many stairs. She didn't know what street they were on and she couldn't find the elevator and she panicked. She couldn't get back into his apartment because she had no key. She would have to stay there all day until he came back from the office.

She pictured herself curled up on his doormat like a little girl and somehow it didn't seem grotesque. He would laugh when he saw her and take her inside. She knew she would be safe. She was tempted, and then she knew she had to get out.

Something that didn't look like an exit door was; it led to a large hall with the elevator in it. This was evidently one of those big old buildings that had been cut up into smaller apartments, which was why the layout was weird. The apartments on his side of the floor had probably once been someone's one huge apartment.

Carol was grateful that it was a self-service elevator, and when she had to pass the doorman she looked straight ahead and walked very fast and did not say good morning.

The street hit her with its light and activity. She realized it was a brilliantly sunny day but Matthew Fitzgerald had never had his windows washed. She also realized she was in midtown and life began to seem real again. She got the first taxi she could find and went home.

When she got home she called her service and he had already called. She called him at his office.

"Do you want to go to an opening tonight?" he asked.

"Okay."

"It's formal, do you mind?"

"No, that's fine."

"I'll pick you up at six. I'll have my car. We can go to the party afterward, or if you don't want to we can go to Twenty-one."

"Or we can do both."

"All right."

Neither of them said anything about the night before. Carol never intended to mention it again and she hoped he wouldn't. Then maybe they could forget they'd done it and could keep on being friends. But she kept remembering the kissing. She would never forget the kissing for the rest of her life.

21

He had his limousine for the opening, but he would never let the driver open the door. He would jump out and open it himself, saying, "Don't get out, don't get out."

The party afterward was very crowded. Carol knew a lot of the people. It was so crowded that Matthew Fitzgerald (she still couldn't think of him by his first name, even after the night before) had to hold her hand so she would not get shoved away and lost. He seemed to like that, and his hand was not shaking, although they had each had only one drink. But except for holding her hand in the crowd he was as formal as he had been before the-night-before. Apparently he wasn't going to mention it either.

"This is boring," he said. "Let's go to Twenty-one."

She wasn't bored, but she followed him out through the crowd. They passed a man she had dated before she became a hermit. He was a super-beauty and Carol restrained herself from mentioning that she knew him. Matthew Fitzgerald would see through that, and she didn't have to prove things anymore. She pretended not to see him.

"I could not possibly eat a chickenburger that costs seven dollars," she said at 21. "So I'll have a steak."

She also had one glass of wine which she could not drink. She felt as if she were choking. She couldn't even smoke. She went to the ladies' room and he gave her a dollar. She brought him back seventy-five cents.

"What's that for?"

"Your change."

"You gave her a *quarter?*" he said. "You're so cheap."

"That's all right, I didn't tell her I was with you."

"You make a lot of money, how can you be so cheap?"

"It's pathological."

He shook his head, but he seemed amused and pleased. "Would you like to keep the seventy-five cents in case you have to go again?"

"All right." She grabbed it. He laughed.

"If I had met you when I was young I'd be a rich man today."

"You are rich."

"I'd be richer."

Coming back in the limousine, he said: "I don't do this, you know. I don't get involved."

"Neither do I."

He took her to her front door and left her there. He didn't kiss her good-night or hint to come up, and she didn't ask him. She was very pleased and relieved at the way he was handling it.

Then why did she spend the next evening sitting by the phone? She began to feel depressed and lonely, and remembered that feeling from college, from later in her early twenties, when she was unformed and silly. She hadn't sat by the phone for years, except for business calls. She never cared if someone didn't call. *Are you going to turn out to be the kind of sick person who only falls in love with someone when he's mean to you?* It was ridiculous; she couldn't even read or watch television. She smoked about a pack of cigarettes. Then he called.

"You sound terrible," she said. "What's the matter?"

"Nothing. I'm just depressed."

"Why are you depressed?"

"I don't know."

"Do you want me to come over and cheer you up?"

"No," he said. "I want to be alone."

"You shouldn't be depressed. It's Saint Patrick's Day. It's your holiday."

"Fuck Saint Patrick's Day."

"Okay. Are you sure there isn't anything I can do?"

"No. I just called to say hello. I'm going to say goodbye now."

"Don't get drunk."

"All right. I won't."

He hung up. She wandered around her apartment and was glad he was depressed. It served him right. That made two of them. She wondered if he was a manic-depressive. Then she took a sleeping pill and went to sleep with the television on for company.

He called the next night and asked if he could come over for a drink. He arrived an hour late, very drunk.

"Last night I finally went to sleep and then I woke up in the middle of the night," he said. "And I realized there's nothing I can do about it: I love you."

"I love you too," Carol said.

"You don't have to love me. It doesn't make any difference. I love you."

He knew even that: that she said "I love you" the way people say "Thank you" for a compliment, just because it was the proper thing to say. She looked at him and thought how safe he made her feel. He was the first man she'd ever known who was a grownup. She could have a normal life with him. He wouldn't keep putting her down because she made him feel insecure. Other people were borrowers; they borrowed your money or your time or your affection and never thanked you for it because they kept pretending they were going to give it back. They couldn't give it back. For once in her life she wouldn't have to worry about making all the decisions for someone else. *He* would take care of *her*. She had to try sometime to make things work out. Was this how the magic choice was made? How did she know? She had never really been in love with anyone.

He kept chasing her around the couch and saying, "I love you." It was like that night in the restaurant. She was getting sick of it. She didn't want him to love her that much, and most of all she didn't want him coming over dead drunk and chasing her around. She was too used to doing the chasing. She was too used to making the decisions. She felt as if she were watching the whole scene from a place slightly away from it.

"It isn't going to work," she said. "This is the high point and from here on it starts to go downhill. Then it gets rotten."

"Where did you get that idea?" He suddenly seemed sober.

"It's always that way," she said.

"You're wrong. You don't know anything. It gets better."

"It gets better?"

"Of course it does. You'll see."

Maybe he was right. She didn't know. She only knew about love getting worse. She didn't even know if she was in love with him or not. But he had said he didn't care and she believed him. She knew that she had been waiting for something to happen to her. Maybe it was all very simple: there was a certain time in your life when you were ready. She did know that this time, with this person, she wanted to try.

22

"You're never home anymore," Randolph said. "I call you at four o'clock in the morning to come to a good party, you're out. I call you at eleven in the morning, and you *never* go out that early, and you're out, which means you're not home yet."

She was visiting him in his apartment because he'd broken his toe and was making a federal case out of it. He was reclining in his black leather and rosewood con-

tour chair with his bandaged foot on the matching otto-
man. He was wearing a bathrobe. The apartment was
full of flowers. There was a girl in the kitchen making
beef stronganoff.

"What have you been up to?" Randolph said.

"Nothing."

"I know you. You're seeing him."

"Who's him?"

"Matthew Fitzgerald. The drunken millionaire who
has no taste at all in movie scripts."

The girl appeared at the doorway of the kitchen. She
was blond and young. "Is she staying for dinner?" she
asked Randolph, not looking at Carol.

"Do you want to stay for dinner?"

"No," Carol said. "I have a date."

The girl went back into the kitchen. "Who's that?"
Carol said.

"Heidi."

"Heidi what?"

"I don't know," Randolph said. "You know I can
never remember their last names."

23

Ellen's husband was working late, so she and Carol had a drink at the Palm Court. Carol was to meet Matthew Fitzgerald at seven thirty at his apartment. He had business drinks every afternoon.

"I have a man for you to meet," Ellen said. "I've never seen him, but he works in Michael's office and he's supposed to be very interesting."

"I've had one of your blind dates."

"Oh, I apologize for him. I never even saw him. But he really did come well recommended. But this one is supposed to be better. Michael knows him."

"The other one gave me colitis."

"I'm really sorry. Have another drink, I'm buying." She waved at the waiter. "He's dying to meet you. We told him all about you."

"I'm sort of going with somebody."

Her face lit up. She was already dreaming of doves in cakes. "Oh, who?"

"Just a nice man. He's married."

"Oh, Carol. What do you want to do that for?"

"I like him."

"Is he unhappy with his wife? Do you think he'll get a divorce?"

"I never asked him."

"You know I only say this because I care about you," Ellen said. "I'm not being nosy, I just care about you. I love you. You're too good for that."

"But not too good for some creep you've never met."

"Well, do you think he's going to marry you, or what?"

"Why is it," Carol said, "that whenever I have an affair with a bachelor none of my dear friends who know me so well ask me if he's going to marry me? But if I go out with a married man, it seems to be life or death to everyone that we get married."

Ellen looked at her in surprise.

"I never thought of it that way," she said finally.

24

"I know you'll be delighted," Carol told Princess Margaret Rose Tenenbaum. "I'm going out with a married man."

"Oh goody! At least now you can be in love with

somebody nice instead of all those young creeps who've been taking advantage of you."

"We've been through a lot of wars together, you and I."

"But we still look young, thank God. I saw a girl I went to high school with at Kenneth. She looked like my mother."

"Married, of course."

"Of course. Twenty children. Foo."

"He's going out of town this weekend," Carol said. "We can have dinner and maybe go to a movie."

"Great. Saturday?"

"Fine."

"Do you think he'll get divorced?" the princess asked.

"No."

"Why not? Married men get divorced all the time."

"But I don't want him to get divorced."

"But if he did get divorced and wanted you to marry him, wouldn't you marry him?"

"I don't want to think about it."

"But why not? If he wants to marry you, why not marry him?"

"I don't want to get married," Carol said. "I don't want to marry anybody."

25

There was a time, a long time in the past when Carol first left the safety of her parents' home, when she could not sleep alone. She had slept alone at home, of course, but with her own apartment came that queen-size bed, and it had seemed enormous. She had lain there in terror, in one little corner, wedded to insomnia till death do us part. Then she met a nice boy who had a crush on her, and invited him to stay. The cure for insomnia is company. He lasted about a year, and after him there was usually somebody. But when she became a hermit everything changed. She began to like her bed. She used both sides of it and the middle. It was all hers. She never wanted to sleep with anyone again. If she ever got married, they would buy the largest king-size bed in the world.

Matthew Fitzgerald had a queen-size bed and Carol could not sleep. He was easy to sleep with: he did not roam around, he kept to his own little corner, he never snored. But he was there. She had trained her mind to resent anyone being there, and even though he gave her three-fourths of the bed, she could never really sleep until he left for the office in the mornings. Then she bolted the door, put on her underpants and his shirt, and slept deeply, like the happy spinster she was. The only problem was that when he wasn't there she had nightmares.

Sometimes she would wake up in the middle of the night from one of her fitful catnaps and find him gone. She would go into the living room and find him asleep on the couch.

"Come back to bed," she would say dutifully.

"You can't sleep with me there."

"Yes I can." She would drag him back to bed.

"You need more sleep than I do," he would say. "I keep you up, jumping on you like a beast."

"You only jump on me about three times a night."

"I can't help it."

She figured it was a phase that would pass. After a while people got used to each other and their sex lives toned down. She might as well enjoy it while it lasted. She wondered who had given him this inferiority complex about being an intruder in his own bed. She knew he and his wife had always had separate bedrooms. When she had asked him why, he had said, "We had so many rooms we figured we should each have one."

Was that one more of the right things that very rich people did, or did it mean something? She was not really interested in his sex life or lack of it with his wife and did not hint to find out. Men lied anyway.

Since Carol slept until noon and it was at least one thirty by the time she dragged herself home, the days went very fast. He always called after lunch to ask her out for the evening. Even though she considered that they were going together, he never took anything for granted. His calling every afternoon for a date was archaic, but she liked it; she was not trapped. She took a clean pair of panty hose in her purse when she went to meet him, and kept no clothes in his apartment. She wore his bathrobes, taking care to roll down the sleeves again when she took them off and hung them up.

"You should keep some things here," he said. "You can't live like a gypsy."

"I don't mind."

"I don't like it."

So she brought a few old things she didn't like anyway, just in case she spilled something on whatever she'd worn the night before, and she never wore them. He took her to the drugstore and bought her all the makeup she used, and a shower cap. She rationalized that it was practical for the weekends when he was in town, because then she did not go home.

He made his own breakfast, washed the one cup and saucer for her, and never made her cook. They had all their meals out. He bought her brand of cigarettes by the carton, although he didn't approve of smoking.

"I can't cook, you know," Carol had told him immediately.

"You don't have to. If I want a cook I can hire one."

"I used to cook. But then I got sick and tired of men who told me I wasn't feminine because I didn't make gourmet dinners. I hate gourmet dinners. I happen to like steak and salad."

"Then I'll hire a cook who makes steak and salad,"

he said. "You never have to do anything you don't want to with me."

"Okay."

"But I wish you'd be more honest. You never tell me what you hate and what you like. How am I supposed to know if you don't tell me?"

"All right, I will."

"You won't," he said. "But I wish you would."

He asked her to find him a maid and she did. Neither she nor the maid had a key. The elevator man gave the maid a pass key which she returned every day when she left.

"Anything we need, call the grocery and charge it," Matthew told Carol. Anything they needed she wrote down on a piece of paper and told the maid to call the grocery and charge it. Carol was afraid if she called the grocery they would ask her who she was.

When Matthew went away on business trips or to see his family Carol stayed in her own apartment. The first night she was always relieved. She could sleep alone in her big bed, and before she slept she could stay up and watch old movies until four in the morning if she wanted to. She missed her former habits. He hated television. At home she cooked for herself with great care: spaghetti with homemade sauce, strange casseroles and stews, sour cream coffee cake, homemade chicken soup. She wrote think-pieces for magazines. They took just long enough to fill the time that he was gone, and the money was good.

But in a week or ten days, when he was due back, Carol found herself missing him. She could no longer sleep well, and if there was nothing she liked on television she felt cheated. There seemed less and less she liked on television.

Matthew phoned her every day from wherever he was. He called station to station and if she wasn't home he called again. Carol knew it was possible to check people's names on telephone bills when you called person to person, and she wondered if that was why, or if it was just his way to be impatient with operators when he could do it himself.

She got him a window washer. It improved the apartment, but he didn't even notice until she called it to his attention.

"I hate this apartment anyway," he said. "I might fix it up or I might move. When I got it I just took the first thing I saw because I wasn't going to spend much time here. I didn't know I would meet you."

"I just wish you had a television set," she said.

He bought a large color television. He used it to watch the six o'clock news. He wasn't making so many drink dates after work; he was coming home early. "I never came home early in my life," he said.

They had drinks together every evening, making a concoction of vodka, diet tonic, and orange juice in his plastic glasses, the kind you didn't have to wash but threw away. Carol washed them.

Matthew had a book that listed all the New York restaurants. They read it every evening and picked a different place to go. He couldn't care less about being seen with her in restaurants. He didn't seem to care what anybody thought about anything.

He kept saying, "I should have a key made for you." She never said anything.

Then one day he said, "Look what I just found when I was cleaning out the bookcase. An extra key." He gave it to her.

"Good," Carol said. "Now I can double lock the door when I leave in the mornings and you won't get robbed."

"There's nothing here to rob," he said.

The grocery he patronized did not carry light bulbs: it was more of a glorified delicatessen. Carol had a thing about light bulbs because she was afraid of the dark. She always slept with a light on in the apartment. He didn't have any extra light bulbs and this made her nervous. She didn't know how long he had owned the ones he had in the lamps. Since she now had her own key she could come and go as she pleased. On a clear spring day she decided to walk around the neighborhood and find a store that sold light bulbs and buy him a supply.

She walked to a five and ten, looked with distaste at the pots and brooms, and bought eight hundred-watt bulbs. It did not occur to her that this would be a trauma; at the moment it simply seemed practical. But walking back to Matthew Fitzgerald's apartment with the light bulbs in a paper bag she suddenly felt as if she were choking. Trapped. A housewife, a housekeeper, a good little mistress who plays house. Carol Prince did not live in men's apartments and buy them light bulbs. Next thing she would be buying sponges and dishrags, and then throw pillows and good dishes and real glasses, and then she would be keeping house. A wife. She was shaking and felt dizzy. She could leave the light bulbs with his doorman and run.

She went into the nearest luncheonette and sat at the counter and ordered chocolate milk. Kid's food, to quiet the shaking. She smoked a couple of cigarettes and took a Librium with the chocolate milk and after a while she felt better. She forced herself to put the light bulbs in his apartment, neatly lined up on a shelf so he would see them, and that afternoon when he called her at home to ask if she could have dinner with him she told him she thought she might stay home and sleep alone because she was tired. She said she would call him later.

She called Paul and Sally. They liked to come into the city at a moment's notice. They decided to meet at Carol's apartment for drinks and then find Armenian food.

They had a lot of wine. Carol had resolved not to tell anybody else about her new affair, but Paul always seemed so solid and wise about things, even though he was younger than she was. Perhaps it was because he had been married a long time and he was getting bald.

"Who is he?" Paul said.

"I can't tell you anything, just that he's married and a good person."

"Where did you meet him?"

"I know him a long time."

Sally didn't say anything, she just started eating candy.

"Does his wife know?"

"Of course not."

"How can she not know?"

"She lives out of town."

"How often does he see you?"

"We sort of live together."

"Then he doesn't go home at night."

"How can he go home at night, she's about five thousand miles away."

"Is he a gangster?" Sally said through a mouthful of caramel. "I love gangsters."

"What makes you think he's a gangster?"

"He's so mysterious."

"He's not mysterious," Carol said. "He's a businessman and he travels."

"He must be rich," Paul said. He seemed less disapproving. "Is he separated?"

"No."

"Do you think he'll marry you?"

"I don't want to marry him," Carol said. Then she told them about the great light bulb trauma.

"I know just what you mean," Sally said. "We've been married eight years and I still feel that way. The other night I came home from work and I had to go to the fish store to get Paul's supper. I was tired and angry and I thought: What the hell am I doing here picking out fillet of sole for my husband's supper when I worked all day and I don't even *like* fillet of sole. And then I had to cook it. I still feel single; I don't think I'll ever get used to being married."

Carol glanced at Paul but he did not seem the least disturbed.

"About once a month I tell Paul I'm getting a divorce," Sally said contentedly. "He doesn't care."

"Sally has to be free," Paul said.

"So you don't think I'm a freak," Carol said.

"No," Paul said. "You seem to be handling it very well."

After dinner when Carol came home she telephoned Matthew. For the first time she was able to think of him by his first name. He sounded angry on the phone and didn't want to talk to her. She thought he was jealous.

The next afternoon he came to her apartment for a drink after work. They sat on the couch together but he didn't talk. He still seemed very angry.

"Look, you're mad," she said. "Tell me why you're mad."

Then he was furious. "You said you would call, and you didn't call until half past twelve. I could have had a date. You ruined my evening. A girl I used to know called and wanted me to go out with her. I hadn't seen her for a long time and I wanted to see her. But I had to stay home and wait for you because you said you would call, and then you didn't."

"I called."

"Half past twelve. And then you said you wanted to stay home."

"You wouldn't talk to me."

"You're selfish. I wanted to see that girl."

"So call her. Call her. We're both free, you said so."

Then just as quickly as he had flared up he wasn't angry anymore. "I didn't care about her," he said. "The truth is I was jealous."

"You didn't have to be. I didn't have a date."

"I was jealous anyway."

"I wish you would never scream at me anymore," Carol said. "It scares me."

"Don't be scared when I scream. Just be scared when I'm very quiet."

"I promise not to stand you up anymore," she said.

"That's all right," he said calmly. "You will."

Before they left to go out to dinner she took a small suitcase with some things in it. He carried it.

"I hope you saw your lousy light bulbs," she said.

"I did. Thank you."

26

September 14, 1958. Patient: Carol Prince, age 26, single. Diagnosis of Rorschach Test: Paranoid Neurotic. The following is a short essay written by patient at Dr. Viderberg's request. Subject: Love. Patient obviously has some talent in direction of writing, not unusual in patients with this psychological problem.

When I think of love I measure it in terms of sacrifice, violence and death. There is no happy ending. My recurring fantasy, which I use to measure how much I love somebody, is always one of two: I have been ship-wrecked with two people I love. I can save only one. Which one will I save? The people struggling in the icy midnight waters of this vast ocean are always my mother and my father, or my mother and my lover, or my father and my lover, or my two imaginary children (a girl and a boy), or my lover (who is my husband in this fantasy) and our imaginary child. There is no happy ending. Whichever one I choose, I must live the rest of my life with sorrow and guilt. My parents are old; suppose I choose my lover? Suppose then, after I have killed my father or my mother, he leaves me? Our child is young and deserves life, but I love my husband more and we can have other children.

Why do I force these terrible choices on myself?

My other fantasy involves Hitler's S.S. troops who have just gathered up a great many of us Jews, among whom is my lover (whether or not he is Jewish does not matter in this fantasy) and myself. The S.S. man tells my lover and me that we have to choose which one of us will be killed. The other one will be saved. My lover wants to die for me. I insist on dying for him. If I let him die for me, I will die of sorrow. If I die for him, how can he live with the guilt of letting me die? There is no happy ending.

27

Carol found small, tender things about Matthew to love. His large, round head, which reminded her of the skull of a four-year-old boy. His thick, shaggy, perfectly cut hair, always smelling faintly of shampoo. His long, football player legs. His clumsy, impatient hands, which could not put in his own collar studs or fold his own turtleneck, but which did things for her; opened jars, fixed doorknobs, carried heavy shopping bags filled with clanking bottles, turned mattresses, fixed broken air-conditioners, and touched her—not clumsily, not impatiently.

Fantasies she had not thought about in years haunted her: the shipwreck and the S.S. troops. She imagined tortures he would gladly undergo to save her. It made her sick with guilt and grief. Sometimes she preferred to think that he would try to kill the S.S. men and die fighting. She did not yet know which was more like him, to suffer or to die. He was a practical man and a brave one, and he was an old street fighter. When he walked on the streets at night his eyes darted, seeing drunks, panhandlers, junkies, muggers, murderers; he walked slowly, holding her arm, but the eyes watched. She felt precious.

In his apartment sometimes she would catch him looking at her with those unreadable eyes and she found sadness in them. "Are you happy?" he would ask.

"Yes."

"I want to make you happy."

"I am."

"Tell me what you want. Tell me what you like."

"I want to be with you," she said. She knew he wanted more of an answer, but she could never think of one. Nobody had ever asked her what she wanted.

She still had her colitis but she never told him. It was not an attractive subject. He knew she ate strangely, but he did not comment on it. People ate strangely. He knew she took pills when she thought he was not watching. He knew she spent a lot of time in the bathroom, but so did other people. He never asked her why she did anything, only what she wanted.

One night Carol was in pain, and he thought she was angry at him. "What is it?" He rocked her like a child. "Tell me."

She told him. She tried to make it sound funny.

"You poor kid," he murmured. "You never say anything. But you have to tell me these things. I understand. Don't be such a loner."

"I'll try," she lied.

"Do you want to see a doctor?"

"No."

"My stomach hurts too when I get upset. Tell me when it hurts, it will make it better. Don't be afraid."

The pain went away, at least for that night.

On Sundays when Matthew was in town they slept late, read the papers, listened to music, and made sandwiches and Bloody Marys for breakfast. Then they would go out for brunch. It was like a child's picnic, an orgy of eating. Carol was happy.

Then one Sunday morning something happened that frightened her and haunted her for a long time.

Matthew was standing at his bar, making a Bloody Mary for her. He made it with great care, measuring just so, adding all the spices delicately, tasting, adding more of this or that, cutting and squeezing the fresh lemon, shaking the concoction in the shaker, finding just the right size glass. He was wearing a mustard-colored jumpsuit, and he looked like a child in its Dr. Dentons, the flesh tender and vulnerable over the smooth muscles. There was a long, lethal-looking knife on the bar. Carol suddenly thought how easy it would be to grab that knife and plunge it into his heart. She could kill him, standing right there making a Bloody Mary for her with love.

She saw it all: his death, and herself standing over him in horror and grief. If she killed him she would kill the only person who had ever loved her for herself.

She felt so sick she had to retreat to the far end of the room and sit on the couch. Love for him, the man whom she had thought of stabbing to death with that long knife, filled and overwhelmed her. She wanted to cry. Why did she want to kill him, when he was the only person she would save in the shipwreck, in the firing squad?

The image came back, over and over, as the weeks went by. She had to figure out why it had happened. Did she hate him? Did she have to kill him to love him? It occurred to her only briefly and in passing that she was crazy. She was too analytical for that. The hateful picture came back again and again, her hand plunging the long, sharp knife into that soft, vulnerable body of the person who loved her most.

That was when she began to be afraid that he would have a heart attack and die in the night. She would stay awake and lean over him in bed, listening for his heartbeat, measuring it for something queer, making sure he was breathing. She could see the headlines: "Mistress found in love nest with dead man." Who would she call? She didn't even know the name of his doctor. Would she have to call his wife? What could his wife do so far away? Carol didn't know his sister's name, or even his parents' first names or where they lived. Would she have to call the police? Should she run?

"Do you have a doctor here?" she asked him.

"Sure. Why?"

"I want to know his name."

"That's silly," he said.

"What if you get sick?"

"Then I'll call him."

"But what if you die?" she said.

"I'm not going to die," he said. "I promise."

"Tell me what all your pills are for in case you need them."

He told her, rather annoyed, and none of them seemed to be much good for imminent death. She started smoking more. At least that way she could die first. Why had she wanted to kill him?

When you open up to someone and start feeling, Carol thought, you really crack right open. You never know what's going to happen.

28

She was curious about his wife and children. He had no pictures of them. He did not even have paintings on the walls, although there were three large picture hooks in the living room, one of which the maid used to hang her coat on. He said the previous maid, who had disappeared, had hung the picture hooks hoping he would get some paintings. Carol told him the next time he went home to bring her a photograph of his children.

He brought it: a girl and a boy, twelve and fourteen. Neat, beautiful, perfect children, standing at attention in the way of children who hate having their picture taken. They both had long, clean, shiny hair. They were wearing school uniforms. Carol wondered if the girl looked like his wife.

She thought about his wife as little as possible. You couldn't start surmising about the unknown third person; then she would become all.

Her friends often asked her what his wife was like. It sometimes seemed they were more interested in his wife than in him. Carol wondered about his marriage. If a husband was almost never home and spent his time with another woman, then it was a failed marriage, was it not, or at least a strange one? Or maybe that was the way very rich people lived, the wives staying home in the mansions with the servants and the children and the cars and the swimming pools, comparing notes about their rotten husbands who were away all the time making money. She seldom asked him about it because he answered her with evasions and platitudes and a pained look that said a gentleman did not betray his honor.

He told her his wife had been a professional lobbyist before their marriage, working in Washington. He had admired her for that job, which was rather unusual for a woman in those days, and for her individuality and brains. When they got married she quit working, and then they had the children. Carol wondered if their marriage had started to fail when she stopped working and became a housewife and mother. Perhaps she became dull to him. She never went with him on business trips anymore; she wouldn't leave the children. She had never seen his New York apartment, or the one in London. She hadn't even been to New York since the oldest was born. When she took the children to their house in the south of France every summer they flew over the Pole.

One night Carol finally asked him if his marriage had begun to die because his wife had stopped working.

"There are a lot of reasons," he said thoughtfully. "But there are never answers."

"Love," she thought, "is never having to say you're sorry."

"If I stopped working, would you hate me?" Carol asked him.

"Of course not. That's not why I love you."

"If I had to go away for two weeks on a story, would you resent it?"

"Of course not. That's what you do."

Carol went to a hotel downtown to interview an underground movie star for a magazine. The star was sitting in the dark with some friends, or her entourage, watching home movies of herself running around naked. Some of the entourage were also in the film, also naked.

"Look," the star said, "there's me, peeing in the pool."

Everybody was smoking pot and drinking wine. The home movies went on forever.

"That's Gar," the star said. "That's me playing with his cock."

Carol fell asleep on the couch. She woke up to the sound of something whirring near her ear and a bright light shining in her face. They were taking home movies of her sleeping. There was also sound. She hoped she had not talked in her sleep.

"You looked so cute asleep," the star said. "If you come back next week you can see it."

It was four o'clock in the morning and Carol went home to Matthew's apartment. He was glad to see her.

Two days later she read in the newspapers that one of the boys who had been in the underground movie star's hotel room had gotten high on LSD and flown off the roof. She must have been sorry not to have filmed that scene, or perhaps she had. Carol did not go back to watch the movie of herself sleeping.

The piece was easy enough to write, but the only problem was that it was very short and the editor complained about having to pay full price. Carol was getting sick and tired of having to fight about money all the time. Why didn't they call her agent; why did they come sneaking to her? There was a time she would have gone back to that boring, sordid hotel room, she would have camped there for a week, brushing off the cockroaches, she would have faithfully recorded every detail of those tiny, unimportant people with their giant egos slobbering over themselves. She just couldn't do it anymore. The hell with all of them.

She wondered if Matthew's wife had entertained hostilities along those lines before she quit her job with relief and became whatever she was now. Carol had no idea what she looked like, but she pictured her. In her fantasy the children were very young, and their mother was bathing them together in a large tub filled with floating plastic balls and rubber ducks. Late afternoon sunlight was streaming in through the window on her hair, making her look young and misty. The children were laughing and splashing in the tub. The governess was making supper in the nursery kitchen. Matthew was not there.

What would his wife do when the children had been

put to bed? Would she drink? Would she listen to music, dancing alone, a cocktail in her hand? Would she watch television? Would she take tranquilizers, sleeping pills? Would she call him then, stoned, lonely?

I know what I would do, Carol thought. I would become a monster.

29

One morning Matthew woke up, looked at Carol sleepily, and said with great tenderness, "Monkey."

"What?"

"You're my monkey," he said, and went back to sleep holding her like a baby.

That was when she became his child. She was already his lover and his best friend, as he was hers, but now she was his child too, and they played children's games: owl, and making faces, and him making her giggle. When his daughter was a baby, standing up in her playpen, he had made faces at her to make her laugh. Now he made them to make Carol laugh. He said when his daughter started school she stopped thinking he was funny; she told him—very dignified with her squeaky voice—that he was silly. He seemed sad about that. It was as if by growing up and moving out of his life she had somehow betrayed him.

It was summer. When Matthew's wife and children went to the south of France he took Carol with him to California. She insisted on staying at a hotel. If she were married she wouldn't want her husband bringing home any girl to shack up in her house. Do unto others. Also she had a fantasy of his wife appearing in the doorway of his bedroom with a gun.

On her interviews Carol had often been on planes with stars and their mistresses. She was fascinated by those thin, beautiful girls in their traveling outfits, their slacks and mink coats, their matched Gucci luggage. She liked the cool way they took out their single girl passports at Immigration, waving offhandedly at the movie star's entourage as they said, "I have seven pieces of luggage, seven. Don't miss any." The movie stars would often be married. Outside the terminal they would crow delightedly about smuggling in a wristwatch. It never bothered them to be smuggling in a mistress. She wondered what those girls did all day—shop, go to the hairdresser, the masseuse, visit friends? They never had jobs. They were free to travel the world. Usually they were divorced. That made them less dangerous: an unfortunate marriage as an eighteen-year-old made them want to stay single. They always said their ex-husbands had been rich. That made it respectable to be kept. Carol decided she wanted to be like them, to be free, to travel with a man she loved, to have someone else to juggle passports and tickets and luggage and hotel reservations, to have cars waiting at airports instead of surly taxi drivers trying to pile her in with four other people who were going to the Hilton. She did not tell anyone she was going to California with Matthew because she did not want them to break in on her fantasy.

They sat in first class, holding hands and sometimes kissing. It was summer, so she could not wear a fur coat, but she was wearing her favorite dress and had had her hair done. As soon as they got into the pressurized cabin it got stringy again. After they took off the stewardess spilled a Bloody Mary on her dress. When they turned the lights out for the movie Carol took off her dress to dry and sat there in her slip. Matthew went right to sleep.

The movie was terrible and the earplugs hurt Carol's ears. She sat there listening to the sound of the engines and thinking. What if the plane crashed? She had never been afraid of a plane crash in her life, but now she wondered what her parents would think when they found out she was dead and they hadn't even known she was away. She didn't want to die. Then she felt herself getting colitis and ducked under the screen to go up front to the bathroom.

She looked in the mirror in the bathroom and she looked awful; green. She fainted.

After a while the stewardess knocked on the door. "Are you all right?"

"No."

They had her sitting in the galley section with an oxygen mask on her face. No one but Carol paid any attention to the fact that she was wearing her slip. The next thing she knew, Matthew came charging in under the screen, looking as pale as she knew she was. He had her ticket in his hand.

"Do you know her?" the stewardess asked.

"Yes," he said.

"Does she have a condition?"

He looked terrified. "I don't know."

Carol pulled the mask off her face. "No," she said, "I do not have a condition." Then she put it back on and wished they would all go away.

"She'll be all right," the stewardess said. "She just fainted."

"I want my dress," Carol said.

When they were back in their seats Matthew still looked distraught. "I nearly had a heart attack," he said. "I thought you were going to die."

"I bet you would have said you didn't even know me."

"I was asleep and the first thing I knew she came back and asked if I knew who you were. I didn't even know you were gone."

"What did you tell her?"

"I said I knew you."

"That was kind of you."

"You looked terrible."

"I felt terrible."

"How do you feel now?"

"Okay."

"When we get to California you're going to my doctor."

"No I'm not," she said.

"Yes you are."

"I am not going to any doctor."

"We'll see," he said.

His house in California was just what Carol had thought it would be. Sunlight poured in on the antiques, which would have shone in the dark by themselves. There were signed photographs of three presidents, in silver frames. Power was apparently non-partisan. That was not what Carol wanted to see: she wanted to see a picture of his wife. There were several, holding the children in various stages of their infancy and childhood, and standing with them now that they were grown. She had been a beautiful woman, and still was, but not as beautiful as Carol had feared. She was very aristocratic looking, like those misty photos taken in the forties by Jay Te Winburn of society women: their fair, straight hair pulled back into chignons (no pompadours for them), straight noses, cool faraway eyes. What a prize she must have seemed to him when he fell in love with her, and how interesting he must have seemed to her.

He did not have just his own bedroom, he had his own suite. So did his wife, and so did each of the children. The house was so big Carol kept getting lost. Mostly she lived by the pool. A boy came to clean it every few days, the gardener came to do whatever gardeners do to flowers, a maid came to clean, and Carol knew they came all the time whether anyone was there or not. There were several cars in the garage and Matthew said she could use one of them, but she could not think of anywhere she wanted to go. Her clothes, the wardrobe she had bought specially for her chic trip as a mistress, hung in the closet of her hotel room. Once more she was a gypsy, her bikini in her purse instead of the clean pair of panty hose, coming to sit by the pool in the sun, changing into a dress in the evening in the hotel room while he met business friends at the hotel bar. After the first day the hotel maid did not bother to unmake the single bed, and after a week she did not even bother to replace the towels. Still, Carol could say she lived at the hotel. If she stayed with him she just happened to be visiting.

His suite in the house overflowed with books. The bookshelves were filled and he piled books on the floor, the desk, the chairs. He had bought them for the boy he had once been who had never had any, and had wanted them. There were magazines, newspapers, journals. There were shelves of phonograph records. There were old television sets that had broken and neither been fixed nor thrown away. There were radios. They worked, and he kept several on at once, in the bedroom, the bathroom, the dressing room, the library. The air-conditioners ran day and night. There was always sound. It reminded Carol of the way she had been before she met him.

He went to the office every morning but came back to have lunch with her, and came by several times during the afternoon. She sat by the pool, covered with suntan lotion, and for the first time in years got a tan. She wore no makeup. She never drank until they went out to dinner. They ate in restaurants, sometimes with his friends, less frequently alone. His friends did not bring their wives.

Once Matthew had couples in for cocktails. Everyone thought Carol was just another guest, or if they did not, they did not show it. They were all very cordial to her, just as the friends of the movie stars had been cordial to their mistresses. The only one who ignored her was Matthew's one bachelor friend. Obviously he was afraid she had been invited for him. It was just as usual as any cocktail party Carol had been to in New York, including the independent bachelor, except the people were better.

It was in that house, during that time, that Carol really started reading. She had never liked reading much, but that upstairs suite was a candy store of books. She read a book every day by the pool. Nothing intellectual, just books that were fun. Novels, detective stories, garbage. Matthew had other books too, but Carol did not read them.

She knew people, but did not call them. They were from the past. They would ask why she was in California, and she would have to decide whether to lie or tell them something they would not be able to resist a comment on. She was tired of comments. She wanted only to exist in the present, as the person Matthew and she had created, this lazy creature who grew more toasty brown by the day, dazed by sun and love.

He wanted her to go to his doctor but she refused. He told and retold to his friends the story of how she had fainted on the plane. After that they knew he was in love with her.

She never knew when they were going to leave, because he planned everything at a moment's notice. She wondered what it would be like to stay there forever, living that way, and she knew it would bore her. It was a vacation, but it could never be her life. Did some women really live that way forever? Of course not; they had children, they became involved in their children's lives, they drove them to school and ballet class and Disneyland. To the dentist and riding lessons and birthday parties and to church. To buy clothes and shoes, to children's plays and concerts and puppet shows. They met other mothers and talked about their children. They had the car fixed. They became boring.

One night Matthew and Carol went alone to a restaurant where neither of them had particularly wanted to go. They had tried all the others and it seemed it might be amusing. It had, he said, mediocre food.

They were sitting on a banquette and had just ordered when a middle-aged man came in alone and sat on the banquette next to Matthew. He looked slightly familiar to Carol.

"Matt!" he said. "What are you doing here? Well, well."

"Arnie Gurney, Carol Prince," Matthew said.

"Hi, honey." She knew he'd had a television show for about ninety-nine years, but she had never watched it, which was why she had not recognized Arnie Gurney. She supposed anyone else would have.

"Family away?" Arnie Gurney said.

"France. They're all fine."

"Mine is here, unfortunately," Arnie Gurney said. "I had to get out of the house, they bore me. Caesar, I'll have the usual, a steak very well done, with catsup and French fried potatoes. Scotch first, a double." He was riveted to Matthew, as if they were having dinner together and Carol was not there. "The show's been renewed again," Arnie Gurney said. "I had to fire the director. He's lost the touch. But I have this good new guy. I was thinking of directing it myself, but I didn't have time, having to watch the writers all the time as it is. My daughter just had another kid. I'm sending them all to Palm Springs for a week or so. It's a shame I hardly ever get to use the house."

"That's nice," Matthew said.

The waiter brought Carol and Matthew's food. Even though they had started eating, Arnie Gurney kept on talking to Matthew, and when the waiter brought his scotch and then the steak he went on, and on, jabber, jabber: obviously Carol was the chick Matt would later bang and should be grateful for the free meal. She tried to think of something to say, but it didn't seem worth the trouble. The fettucini lay on her plate like a lump and tasted like library paste. She couldn't swallow. The meal went on for hours. She wanted to leave, or at least to tug at Matthew's sleeve the way she ordinarily would have done and say, Hey, talk to me. But she sat there, waiting to see what he would do.

Arnie Gurney's flat eyes passed over her and away again. "I like my girl to wear a black lace negligee," he said to Matthew. "She's always wearing it when she waits for me. And black stockings. I like to take them off of her. Black stockings make me hot. She's twenty-eight, but she has a great body."

Matthew didn't say anything. Carol thought how

millions of people loved Arnie Gurney, the lovable family man on their TV set every week, and how surprised they would be to hear him now. It did not surprise her. He was no more or less than many of the lovable celebrities she had interviewed. She thought how surprised he would be to know that the lady of the evening sitting next to his friend was a reporter.

"Coffee?" Matthew said to her.

"No."

He signed the check. "Good-bye," he said to Arnie Gurney. "I'll give your regards to the family."

"Bye, Matt. Keep your pecker up. So long, honey."

Go fuck yourself, Carol said to him in her head.

On the street in front of the restaurant, waiting for the boy to bring around the car, she started to shake. She was like a fox terrier in an elevator, or some spastic. Her teeth were chattering.

She couldn't stop shaking in the car, and then unexpectedly she began to cry. She never cried in front of anybody. She cried now for every time she had never cried, for every time she had been subjected to somebody like Arnie Gurney and had not been able to tell them off, to tell them to get off her back and shut up. She cried because of Matthew, who had failed her.

He pulled over to the side of the road. It was dark, suburban. "Don't cry," he said. "What's the matter? Don't." She couldn't answer, or stop crying either, so finally he started the car again.

"You're ashamed of me," Carol said.

He stopped the car again. "What do you mean, ashamed of you?"

"He thought I was some whore."

He was genuinely astonished. "I thought you knew about him. He's the most repulsive man in Hollywood. I thought you'd find him amusing."

"You let him treat me like some whore."

"Stop crying. Please. He treats my wife the same way. She won't have him in the house. He treats everybody like that. He doesn't know anybody's alive except himself."

He started the car again and drove home very fast. When they got to the house she was still crying. "Carol, please," he said, the unreadable eyes now very wide and filled with pain and fright. "Carol, don't do this to us." It was the only time he had ever called her Carol. "Carol, don't do this to *us*."

She stopped crying. She lay on the bed and felt the nausea beginning, wondering if it would stop. Then she went into the bathroom and threw up.

She threw up everything, the shrimps, the fettucini, Arnie Gurney's rat face, his arrogance, his girl with the black lace negligee and the black stockings. Matthew hovered around her, and cleaned up afterward. She let him.

She lay on the bed listening to him running water in the bathroom and wondered if those chic young mistresses on those airplanes cried when they were alone. She didn't want to be them anymore.

Matthew came out of the bathroom. "Are you mad at me?"

"No," Carol said.

"I love you."

"I know."

"I will always love you, if you want me to. I'll love you anyway, even if you don't love me. I want to be with you forever."

"I love you too," she said. "He just made me sick."

He smiled, relieved. "Our first fight," he said happily.

Afterward he told all his friends how Carol had met Arnie Gurney and he had made her throw up. They were all delighted at this comment on the man no one could stand. After a while Carol almost began to believe the story herself.

30

When they got back to New York they started looking for a new apartment for Matthew. He wanted something bigger, nicer, with a view. He wanted Carol to live with him. She had no intention of living with him, but she liked looking for apartments because she could snoop into the lives of the people who lived there. She was always surprised at how people could buy and cherish such ugly things in their homes.

"I want some place where we can entertain our

friends," Matthew said. "You ought to see your friends more. You never have anybody over. You're so lazy."

"Okay."

"Well, you don't have to if you don't want to. I'm selfish, I have such a good time being with you that I don't want to be with anybody else. But there are people I should have over for drinks, and you shouldn't drop your friends."

"I didn't drop them. I never saw them before either."

"Then you should see them now. I want you to have a normal life."

They finally found an apartment they both liked, and decorated it together. There were no antiques. It was clean and bright and young. They ravaged the stores.

"I never did this before in my life," he said. "I never left the office to buy furniture."

"Who decorated your houses?"

"A decorator."

Matthew signed the lease and spread the proper money around. Carol got the locks changed and had keys made for him and her and the maid and the super. Moving men came to the old apartment and took two crates of clothing (Matthew's), the color TV, the tape machine and tapes, two bottles of vodka, twelve bottles of diet tonic, and an opener for wine. Carol took her makeup. They left everything else.

Moving took exactly two hours. That night Carol and Matthew slept in their new (king-size) bed in their new (modern) apartment, and the next morning they left for Europe.

31

They stayed in his apartment in London, his hotel
suite in Paris, a hotel suite in Madrid. He was out every
morning at half past eight for business meetings, break-
fasts, lunches, conferences. She called people she knew,
met them, shopped. They saw his friends, the husbands
and the wives. They went to dinner parties given by
his business acquaintances. They saw her friends together, like a couple. The difference in attitude was
that Carol's American friends were surprised Matthew
and she had lasted so long, while their European friends
were surprised at nothing. The wives came to the hotel
to take her shopping; they took her to little boutiques
they knew, where everything was an amazing bargain.
The mistresses took her to famous shops where everything cost too much, and she bought nothing while
they bought everything. Matthew never paid for Carol's
clothes; it was not his style or hers.

When they came back from Europe she had several
suitcases filled with all the junk people take on trips
and bring back, and she took it all to his new apartment, which he kept calling Our Apartment. Carol still
did not consider that she lived there, although she

went home only once a week to collect the mail. She was busy in his apartment. She had to sleep till noon, and then she had to write notes for the maid and go to the grocery. She had to be sure his suits went to the cleaner and came back. She had to telephone her friends every day to check in, just like a wife.

"Where are you?" Ellen asked. "His or yours?"

"His."

"What do you do all day?"

"Sit around like a lazy tart. But if you had seen this tart running to the grocery to return a grapefruit they sent with a hole in it. . . . The doormen all call me Mrs. Fitzgerald. It's very embarrassing. At first I didn't know they were talking to me and I didn't answer. It makes me feel schizo. If you could hear that Irishman at the grocery saying, 'Top o' the morning, Mrs. Fitzgerald.' I want to tell him, 'Stop it, I'm Jewish.' But it makes him give me better service thinking I'm a relative."

"I never met anyone like Matthew," Ellen said.

"Neither did I."

"I really like him," she said. "Michael and I both do."

Ellen never asked Carol anymore if he was going to marry her.

"Doesn't he ever work?" Princess Margaret Rose Tenenbaum asked. "Every time I call you he's home from the office already."

"That's because he's there at eight o'clock in the morning."

"Well, he certainly is weird," she said. Her married boyfriend worked late at night, that's how she was able to see him. "Tell Matthew if he ever wants me to work for him I'll be delighted. I love his hours. But I want to come in at ten."

"He has a staff."

"That's all right. Let him fire somebody."

She never asked Carol anymore either if he was going to marry her.

"I'm not going to talk to you," Randolph said.

"Why not?"

"Because you never want to see me unless he's out of town."

"I never saw you pass up a date for me, and you don't even like them."

"You're supposed to be my friend," he said.

Randolph had gone into group therapy to find out why he couldn't fall in love and get married. He announced with pride after the second session that there was a girl in the group whom he had bravely refrained from banging, even though she wanted him, too. The therapist had told him to find a hobby, so he was taking up photography. Nude girls, Carol suspected. She could never think of anything to say to him anymore. She did not give him Matthew's home phone number. She had her own phone. It was a relief to know that the phone was ringing in her own apartment, capturing only her answering service: all the people she couldn't stand, couldn't remember, the mistakes she had made, the guys she'd spent one night with who disappeared for a year, the girls she hardly knew who'd broken up with someone and wanted her to find them a date, the fund raisers, the protest marchers, the friend of a friend from out of town, her mother. Lonely people collected too many strays. They should change their phone numbers at least once a year.

She had slipped quietly from the role of mistress to that of wife. She made diet jello. She was always home when he got there. She changed the soap in the shower when it got too small. She arranged flowers, although not too well. She read books. She also took to reading women's magazines. Whenever they had compatibility tests to judge your mate she took them. She was astonished at the stupid questions they asked. It cheered her to know that married people could be so miserably incompatible. Her score with Matthew was always one hundred percent.

"I have to see my parents," Matthew said one day. "You don't have to come if you don't want to. It will probably be very boring to you."
"I'd like to meet them."
"They're boring."
"So are mine. If I can stand them I can stand yours."
"We won't stay for dinner, we'll just have drinks."
"Okay."
His sister and her husband were having her parents to dinner. Matthew didn't bother to tell them he was bringing Carol.
If anyone was surprised to see her they didn't show

it. His parents both stood up when Matthew and Carol came into the room. They were small and old and looked shy. His sister looked just like Matthew in drag. It was scary. Put a lady's wig on him, paint him up, and there she'd be. Carol would have known her anywhere.

Carol asked for sherry in a small voice. She hated sherry. She was very careful to put her cigarette ashes into the ashtray instead of the coaster.

"Don't you like your drink?" his brother-in-law said.

"Carol doesn't drink," Matthew said.

"Prince?" his father said. "What kind of name is Prince? English?"

"She's Jewish," Matthew said.

"I knew a man named Prince once," his father said. "Or maybe it wasn't—"

"Matt," his mother said, "why don't you take your jacket off?"

"I'm all right," he said.

"No, take it off. It's hot in here."

"I can't, Mom. I don't have a shirt on. This is just a dickey."

"That's all right," she said. "Take it off anyway. We're family."

Matthew took his jacket off, and revealed his long-sleeved, French-cuffed, handmade, monogrammed shirt. His mother smiled at having been fooled. Carol had the feeling he had been putting his mother on all his life, and she had always fallen for it and found it funny. He ran his hand through her gray hair. "My mother has very thin hair," he said.

Carol was embarrassed, but his mother wasn't. She

smiled at him. Carol looked at his thin-haired mother and bald father and said, "How come you've got all that hair?"

"I'm adopted," he said.

His mother smiled at him. Carol liked her. She had the feeling his mother liked her, too.

"My mother is seventy-five years old," Matthew said.

"Seventy-four," his mother said.

"Seventy-eight," his father said. "She lies about her age."

"I've never been seventy-eight," his mother said. "I'm seventy-four." She looked down at her hands with pride. They were old, tired hands, but strong. "I can still clean the house. I washed the kitchen floor this morning. On my hands and knees. As long as I can still work I'm not old."

Matthew kissed her on the cheek. Carol wanted to. She was little and proud and tough and humble. Carol could see Matthew in her.

"Maybe Carol would like some wine," his sister said. "I have some open in the icebox."

"That would be nice," Carol said.

His sister brought her a glass of wine and sat down next to her. "I have a great guy for you to meet," she said. "He's handsome and dashing and rich. He just got divorced. He's forty, is that too old for you?"

"Shut up," Matthew said to her. "Leave her alone."

"You were a skunk not to bring me anything from Europe," his sister said to him. "You never tell me when you're going away. The next time I have a list of things I want."

"You're not getting anything," Matthew said.

"Why not?"

"Because you try to fix Carol up with old men."

Carol sipped the wine, kept her legs crossed at the ankle, and restrained herself from lighting another cigarette.

"You ought to get my father started telling you stories about the old days in Ireland," Matthew said to her. His father didn't say anything. He wasn't listening. Her father didn't listen either. Carol felt comfortable with Matthew's father too, as if they were related. If her father had met Matthew he would have tried to think of somebody named Fitzgerald he had met, or any Irishman in fact. Carol didn't think he knew any.

"The thing I remember most," Matthew's mother said, "is the funerals. We had these long wakes, you know. It's like a party. I remember when I was a girl they used to pack the body in ice so it would keep, and there it was melting ice all over the living room floor."

"I remember Grandma's funeral," Matthew's sister said. "It was beautiful."

"It was terrible," Matthew said. "They had two candles burning, one at her head and one at her feet. Pop made me kiss her good-bye. There was a big blob of wax on her forehead where it had dripped down, and I screamed."

"You did not," his sister said. "You kissed her."

"I didn't kiss her. I screamed and kept looking at that blob of wax."

"She didn't have any wax on her forehead," his sister said. "I remember. You were too young to remember."

"How can I be too young to remember if you're younger than I am?"

"I'm telling you, there was no wax."

"At least they had embalming by then," his mother said. "They don't use ice anymore. It was a mess, putting ice around them for all those days."

"We bury them right away," Carol said. "Bang, into the ground."

"That's more sensible," his mother said. "Do you have a wake after?"

"Sometimes we sit shiva. We eat a lot."

"We drink," Matthew said. He went to the bar and made himself another drink.

"I think our way is barbaric," his sister said. "Your way sounds like more sense."

When they left Carol shook hands with Matthew's father and brother-in-law, and his mother kissed her good-bye. Carol kissed his sister too, because she looked just like Matthew.

"My mother likes you," Matthew said to her on the street.

"I like her."

"When you went to the bathroom she said to me, 'She's very young, isn't she? Is she your secretary?' I said, 'No, she's a reporter.' She said, 'That little girl?' "

"I guess to her I look like a little girl."

"You are a little girl."

"What makes you think she likes me?"

"She told me. She's a smart old lady, my mother. She knows about us, but she'd never say anything to me."

"Doesn't she like your wife?"

"She's crazy about my wife. That doesn't stop her from liking you. My family doesn't interfere with people's lives. We never have."

"Funny, all those stories about the wakes and the ice," Carol said.

"Oh, my father could tell you such wonderful stories. I'm sorry he wasn't on tonight."

She never did get to hear the wonderful stories about the old days, because before she ever saw his father again he was dead.

32

Matthew's flesh was crunchy and chewy as an apple; he smelled like milk. Carol wanted to devour him. He wanted to devour her. How happy he looked when she called him, running to her. How happy she was to hear his key in the lock, the anticipation flowing in with that sound. They had to be touching each other all the time, and when they were not touching, each watched the other in secret (crossing the room, moving to the closet) and they would catch one another at it.

"What are you looking at?"

Then they would rush to each other's bodies with the total lust born of the confidence of love.

It was time to renew her lease. Carol did so, without

mentioning it to Matthew, and let them paint because it was free. She had to have a home. Where would she live if anything happened to him? Mrs. Fitzgerald would simply disappear from his apartment building and never be seen again. The doormen could think she committed suttee for all Carol cared. It was a strange feeling to exist and yet not to exist. But if she were an existentialist she could say that we all exist in each other's minds anyway.

Matthew's wife, the real Mrs. Fitzgerald, existed, but Carol tried not to let her exist in her mind. It was pointless to try to imagine the sound of her voice, the way she looked walking down the halls of that great house. Carol did not want to see her in candlelight sitting at their dining room table entertaining their friends. It seemed an invasion of his wife's privacy to try to imagine her at all.

A friend of Princess Margaret Rose Tenenbaum's flipped out. She was banging her head against the wall and screaming and they took her away. She had been going with a married man. "He didn't love her enough to leave his rotten wife," the princess said. To the princess, a wife was a rotten wife. Her boyfriend had a rotten wife. Carol would not let anyone ever say to her that Matthew had a rotten wife. She was a good woman for whom the system failed. That was all.

Carol was visiting Sally and Paul. Paul was in the yard feeding the Saint Bernard. "I think Matthew is going to marry you," Sally said.

"Why?"

"He can't go on this way. A marriage doesn't go on

like that. His marriage is over. He's going to have to realize it or else you two will break up. You'll get married or it will be over."

"If we're getting along now, why should we break up?"

"That's how things are."

"You think he'll leave me?"

"No. I think he'll leave her."

"Why does anybody have to leave anybody?"

"That's how things are."

"Why do people always think things have to be 'how things are'?" Carol said, annoyed.

"You'll see," Sally said.

I suppose she thinks she's being nice, Carol thought.

33

In December Carol and Matthew had a catered dinner at home (his apartment) with champagne and caviar, and exchanged wedding rings for Christmas presents. "Now we're married," he said.

They carried their rings in their pockets. His didn't fit, anyway. Carol had bought it because it was pretty, and didn't care about the size because she knew he would never wear it. She didn't like men in wedding rings. She had found that the ones who wore them were more apt to cheat, under the illusion that forewarned is forearmed. She didn't want to wear a wedding ring because she didn't want people to think she was married. In stores when she was charging things the salesperson always said, "Mrs.—?" with the pen poised over the charge pad, and Carol always said, "Miss." She liked them knowing she paid her own bills.

The day after Carol and Matthew got "married" he went home to see his wife and children for the holidays, and she went to the stomach doctor to see why she was always sick. It seemed a funny way to spend a honeymoon. She trotted around to labs, swallowed potions, gave them blood and assorted specimens, answered questions, paid vast bills, and finally got the diagnosis: nerves. She could have told them that. She also received some pills, which cured her.

"Think of yourself as a person who has a headache and takes an aspirin," the doctor said. "When you get spasms, take a pill."

When Matthew came back to New York they both decided to stop drinking. They would drink only white wine. They bought books on wine and read about it. Although he traveled the world and ate at only the best restaurants he had never been a gourmet. Rich food made him sick. He liked ham and cheese sandwiches, and bacon and eggs. He liked Carol's chicken soup. She was glad, because no one else would touch it.

People started telling them how beautiful they

looked. Her friends said how calm she had become. His friends said how relaxed he seemed. It was not because they had stopped drinking; it was because they were happy. Carol never spoke to Randolph anymore, but if she had he certainly would have been surprised at what had happened to Matthew, his alcoholic.

They began going to museums, theater, movies. "It's amazing how much time you have to do things when you're not drinking," Matthew said. "Business drinks are a waste of time; I can see those people at the office."

They had been together how long now . . . a year? Carol was not sure which was their official anniversary, the day they had met or the day they started sleeping together. She asked Matthew which he preferred and he said definitely, "The day we went to bed together." She didn't want to celebrate their year together because she was superstitious. A year was a round number, it could mean the end of an entity. She wanted their anniversary to come and go as fast as possible. She was nervous all day, waiting for them to have a fight. He seemed nervous too. They had always put aside the conventional things, so putting too much emphasis on one of them seemed to her to be courting disaster. Matthew had less difficulty than she did in making his own rules, but still, the conventions seemed to make him as irritable as they did her.

They spent most of their anniversary in bed. Another of Carol's myths had quietly vanished: the myth that physical love reaches its peak in the beginning and then goes away.

"We'll always have this," Matthew said. "And we

have everything else. This will get better and better. So we'll go on forever and be happy. I want to make you happy. That's all I want. I just want to make you happy."

They had survived their anniversary. They were surviving time. They knew each other, they were comfortable together, they laughed, they could confide. Neither of them had the slightest physical interest in anyone else. It was all working.

34

But how long had it been since she had worked? What had happened to that part of her? Was this the price you had to pay for being happy?

Growing up in the 1930's and 1940's, and coming into the world as an adult in the 1950's, Carol had always been faced with The Choice. Was she to be feminine, or a ball-breaking career woman? It had to be The Choice. Even before her mother and her boyfriends put it into words, her unattractive, bitter school teachers lived The Choice for her to see.

She remembered all this now, living with Matthew, and she felt as if some mystical curse had been put on her which said, You can never be happy. You can have success and fulfillment in your work or success and fulfillment in love, but never both.

It was something she had heard all her life, she had not invented it. You can't have happiness in everything: the Puritan Ethic. Maybe this was why she used to have fantasies of either her lover or herself being killed by their capturers.

Happiness with Matthew made her superstitious, being away from her work made her depressed. She tried to live The Choice. She cleaned Matthew's apartment when the maid was off. *Why am I cleaning his house, when I don't even clean my own house?* She looked for little things to talk about, to be amusing. The hippie down the hall, whose music she heard through his closed door all day, took on a fascination. He smoked so much pot the hall carpets reeked of it. Did he have orgies? How did he pay his rent? The apartment next door with the young girls coming in and out; was it a brothel for teen-agers? The couple on the other side who fought noisily; would they kill each other? Carol looked for scandal, for vice, for murderers. She looked for anything. Her head became a village, populated by strange people. She averted her eyes in the elevator.

The shopping list for the grocery grew longer, but she never cooked anything but jello. The kitchen was filled with stale crackers, molding cheese, sprouting potatoes. Cooking meals for Matthew would not solve her problem.

There was a color television set in every room, there was a hi-fi, records, tapes. She played the radio all day. She washed the ashtrays and filled them up again. She walked in the streets and wondered where the people were going.

The apartment was decorated, completed. There was not even a cocktail napkin to be bought. Carol had as many clothes as she wanted. She didn't like to go to a gym. She didn't like to go to the movies alone because she was tired of sex fiends sitting next to her.

"You should work on something," Matthew said to her.

"I know."

"Why don't you call that agent of yours and get an assignment?"

"I will."

She called her agent who set up a business lunch. Carol went without him. The editor was a woman, and after discussing several ideas the one both she and Carol liked the best was the idea of Carol spending a few weeks in a commune in the country in Pennsylvania to see what this new fad was all about. They shook hands after the lunch and Carol said she would let her know, but they were both excited and pleased.

When she told Matthew that night he didn't say anything. He just shut her off. He looked elsewhere, he started arranging his papers for the office.

"Well, what do you think?" she said.

"I think you should do what you want."

"What do you really think?"

"You don't really want to know."

"I do want to know," Carol said. "When you ignore me and look grouchy it's the same as saying it, so why don't you spit it out and we'll both feel better?"

"I think that agent of yours is a horse's ass," Matthew said angrily.

"Why?"

"To get you an assignment like that. It's beneath you."

"He didn't get it for me, he just set up the lunch. I got it for myself. I thought it was interesting, I still do."

"What do you want to be with those people for?" Matthew said. "You're a respected writer, you don't have to live with kooks and losers and bedbugs in the woods. A bunch of misfits, neurotics, everybody stoned all day. That's for a beginning writer. You should be interviewing the President."

"He's been done," she said. But she was flattered.

"Your agent ought to get you better assignments, and if he doesn't then you should fire him and get somebody else."

"Well, he doesn't even know about this yet. I wanted to think about it."

"When did they want you to go?"

"As soon as possible."

"I'll be going to Europe in a few months. Why don't you get something in Europe? Then we can be together, and your trip will be all paid for."

"Since when did you suddenly start to worry about money?" she said. "Tell me the truth. If I go away without you, you'll miss me."

"You have to make your own decision," he said.

"Tell me the truth."

"Of course I'll miss you," he said.

Sneak, she thought. Blackmailer. But she was pleased that she was so important to him.

"I really do think that piece is beneath you," he said. "I don't want you to have to work so hard on something like that. If it was something better, I'd be glad for you."

"Then I won't do it," Carol said. "I'll do something else."

He smiled. He looked very happy and relieved.

"It's so stupid for us to be away from each other when we have so little time together," he said. "Talk to your agent about something in France. You have plenty of time to find something."

"And if I can't?"

"If you're good," Matthew said, "I'll take you with me anyway."

35

After Carol phoned the editor to tell her she had decided not to go to the commune, a sort of inertia set in. A few other magazines called with think-pieces, but she could not think; at least not about those subjects which suddenly seemed so trivial. She had her choice: How To Get a Man, How To Keep a Man, or Why You Don't Need a Man. Anything else was a research piece.

Every day when Matthew came home from the office he asked her what she had done all day and she said, "Nothing." Since he usually said he had done nothing and didn't mean it, this did not alarm him. He didn't think she was boring. She did. All he wanted was for her to be happy, and if she was happy doing things she categorized as nothing, that was fine with him.

With the inertia came the nightmares. Carol forgot them in the morning, but it didn't matter, there would always be new ones the next night. She knew wives who worked. Ellen worked. Sally worked. She could get a job. But she never did. She was a journalist; that was her job.

"I don't know, maybe I should get a job," she told Matthew.

"You should get up early in the morning and just sit at the typewriter and write things down," he told her. "All your ideas. It doesn't have to be any good. Just so you do something."

She started getting up early, but she did not buy a typewriter ribbon. The one she had was dried up. So was her head.

She found out through the grapevine who had been assigned the piece on the commune that she had turned down. It was not a girl she would think of as a beginning writer, or even a second-string writer. But she usually got the pieces Carol turned down, that was true. Maybe Matthew had been right. Still . . . if she had done the piece . . . it might have turned out to be her best. There was no point in thinking about it; it wasn't hers anymore.

Then one day her agent called and said there was a job open as the book reviewer on a monthly magazine. Nobody wanted it because you had to read about twenty books a month. The pay was insulting. He had only called to mention it because after all he was her agent and it was his job to report offers to her, no matter how undesirable. She wanted it.

He told her she would have a nervous breakdown if she took it. She told him to accept it on a month-to-month basis in case she did. She could see him thinking that fifty dollars a month commission from a client who was trapped reading twenty books a month meant he had as good as lost a client. She could see herself happily immersing herself in other people's ideas, having something to write about, being busy, being alive again. She didn't have to do it forever, but she could do it until she got her head straight. They needed someone right away and Carol told him she could start the minute the first books came.

"You're crazy," her agent said.

"I need free books," she said. "I just built book-shelves."

The books came to her apartment, so every morning she got up as soon as Matthew left and rushed home to work. Her head was filled with the fantasies of other people's minds, and there was always something she wanted to say about it afterward. She felt like a person again. She was a fast reader, and she arranged everything so she could be back at the apartment when Matthew came home. He was delighted that she was working at something she liked. He took his own clothes to the cleaner, and Carol let the maid fend for herself without her notes. Everything went smoothly; Carol really hadn't been needed as a housekeeper after all. She could still make diet jello at night—so could a first grader.

"Believe me," Matthew said, "whether or not I have jello is not one of the important problems of my life."

She was happy again. Perhaps she had never been happier.

36

The fights started suddenly, for no reason. It seemed to Carol the inevitable phase of a relationship between a man and a woman: the battle of wills. This was the phase that had always broken up her affairs, but in all of them it had come much sooner. She was not used to fighting; a fight meant *finished*. One big fight and out. She knew she had a sharp tongue and had always been careful of what she said in anger because she knew those things were not easily forgotten. The better you knew someone the easier it was to strike to the heart. Too bad Matthew didn't feel the same way—he liked to get it all out, and then like a child was relaxed and happy after he had wished her dead. It never occurred to him that she would always remember he had said it.

They went to the Riviera and fought in all the pretty places. Carol had taken a month off from her job. She was sick: they fought. She was tired: they fought. If Matthew went out for a business drink with somebody, she would lie on the bed fully clothed and find two hours later that she had been asleep.

"I do not want to spend my time here watching television while you sleep," he said nastily.

"Then I'll get up."

"Never mind."

She would get up, groggy and stupefied with heat, take a shower to wake herself, rushing, nervous, afraid he would leave, hating him.

"I can always go out with my friends," he said. "I have friends here."

"Wait a minute, will you? I'm almost ready."

"It's too late. We lost our reservation."

"I didn't know you made one."

"You told me to."

What difference did it make who forgot? She should have been ready, gracious, dressed and prettily made up, waiting for him like a dog.

He even resented her European friends. The girls, he said, were bums, and the men he considered all her old lovers anxious to resume courtship, orgies, who knows what? Carol never worried about his former girl friends and she resented his jealousy.

Matthew invited a friend business acquaintance for drinks in their suite. The two of them talked about business and Carol thought it was dull. They planned a lunch date for the next day with someone else and she was not invited. So she excused herself and went into the bedroom to phone a friend and make a lunch date for herself. Matthew came into the bedroom while she was talking and made gestures for her to get off the phone. She was flattered and smiled at him. He went back to his friend. When she got off the phone the man was gone.

"Where's your friend?"

"He left because you were so obviously bored and it embarrassed him."

"I wasn't bored."

"You looked bored."

"You were talking business. Business is privileged information. I thought I should leave."

"I want you to be interested in my business."

"Well, you never tell me. You never tell me the ground rules. How am I supposed to know?"

"You're supposed to know."

"How? How am I supposed to know?"

"If I invite someone up for drinks I want you to be part of the conversation. If I didn't want you to be there I'd meet him in the bar. You're so insecure the minute you heard I had a lunch date you had to run make one of your own."

"Well, what do you expect me to do, stay in the room and wait for you?"

"Meeting your old boyfriends."

"He's not my old boyfriend."

"Maybe you'd like to move to another hotel. Then you could do what you wanted."

"Don't get paranoid."

"Maybe we should go home."

"That won't solve anything."

What were the ground rules? She wasn't sure she wanted to know. She had never lived by rules and she was sure whatever they were they would all be on his side. She wondered if all love affairs ended like this, with rules and subjugation.

Or maybe there weren't any rules. Maybe he was just a grouch, and that was what his wife knew and she did not. Maybe he was hard to live with and the honeymoon was over. Carol was glad when they went back to New York.

Sometimes, in New York, he would look at her oddly and say in surprise, "You're a stranger. I thought I knew you, but I don't."

She wouldn't answer.

"You think you know all about me, but you don't," he would say.

"I never said I knew you."

"You're supposed to try. You don't try, you don't even care."

"I try."

"You're so sure of me," he said one day. "You think I'm dull. I bet you didn't know that all the time I was taking you out, before I ever made a pass at you, I was having an affair with someone. Those nights I used to take you to dinner, I had a girl waiting for me in my apartment."

"What did you tell her?" Carol said.

"I told her I had to go out."

"Poor girl," Carol said sadly, and meant it. "What happened to her?"

"She called me for a long time. I told her I was busy. Finally I told her I had someone else. She said when I broke up with you I should call her again."

"And—?"

"She finally gave up. There were several of them. They all finally gave up. So there, you see, I had a life too before I met you. You don't know anything about me."

She bit her lip. She remembered how she had thought when he called that he was lonely, that she was just a girl to go out with because he missed his wife. Obviously he had made arrangements long before he met her. He was not the single-minded drone he had pretended to be. She supposed she should resent it but she was rather flattered. He had left another girl for her because she intrigued him. But he had been lonely. Nothing could change that, not a hundred girls waiting for him in that rat hole he used to live in. If he was happy with his wife, he wouldn't be lonely, and if he had been happy with that girl or those girls, then he wouldn't have been lonely, and it was the loneliness she had seen and recognized—nothing could change that.

"You're laughing at me," he said.

"No. I'm just smiling."

"You're crazy. They're going to put you away."

"I wouldn't be surprised," Carol said, and laughed. "But I'll have you to keep me company."

"I won't come to visit you."

"You'll be in there *with* me."

"I'll ask for a different cell, a different floor."

So the fight would be over. They would not admit it, but they knew, gave each other signals, and went on as before. But she had to find out what he wanted of her. She had to find out what he was thinking. She felt disaster hanging over her head. If he wanted to get away she had to know it.

They had one more fight, a ferocious one, which they both wanted. They led up to it, baiting each other, drinking vodka, which they had not had for a long time, trying to get mean drunk and succeeding. He said it was over, that she had never loved him, that she did not care about anything but herself and her work. Carol wondered if it was true. She could not deny it to him, although he was waiting for her to deny it, and that made him furious. If she had never loved anyone, she was thinking, then how could she be so sure she loved him?

She thought of jumping out the window; it would serve him right. But what if he really loved her still and it was not over? What good would it do her then

[195]

to be dead? Crazy people killed themselves. Lonely people only thought about it.

The day after the fight Matthew tried to be kind. But she remembered him saying sadly, "I loved you so much." Loved. She hadn't been cruel, he had. He went home to see his family. Carol wondered if she would ever see him again.

She knew Matthew: he would throw away the apartment and everything in it if love was gone. He collected material things with the delight of a Midas, but they didn't mean anything to him.

Just before Matthew left he took a piece of string and a pair of scissors and measured her wrist. She had mentioned once that she wanted a bracelet. She knew this was his way of saying the fight had not meant anything, but she knew how easy it was to lose a small piece of string. She imagined him finding the string in his pocket and wondering what it was, and throwing it away. "I loved you so much."

37

Carol figured Matthew would call when he had been away for about three days. To be safe, she would give him five. She planned her life, saw her friends, went to movies. She slept twelve hours every night and worked in bed, filling up ashtrays, wallowing in her own dirty apartment. She tried to imagine what life would be like without him. It would never be quite the same as it had been before: she was not really the same person. She had let herself love and feel and be vulnerable, and now she knew more who she was. She was still an independent and stubborn person, but she also knew she was sometimes afraid. She liked herself more now.

She remembered other men, other times, and they all seemed selfish children compared to Matthew. Because they were the men she met they seemed to be the men who were in the world, and therefore she used them as they used her, for companionship, sex, to have somebody. Not to appear alone, unwanted, unloved. They had always said they loved each other because that was part of the morality they had grown up with: you can't pet unless you're going steady.

She had known Matthew for two years; she would be forty soon. Forty and alone. So what? If she lived to be fifty she would think forty was young. She had always rather looked forward to being a mean old lady getting her own way. All her childhood she had wanted to grow up, to be older, so she could do what she pleased without people telling her she was wrong. She would enjoy her forties. She didn't know how, or what she would do, but she would try.

Matthew phoned two days after he had left. Carol was surprised. They were polite and friendly and neither of them mentioned love. She kept on thinking about her future life as if he had not called. It was a relief not to fight with him. Whenever she started to miss him she remembered their fights and then she realized she was afraid of their being together. Being alone was peaceful. At least she was not afraid of their fights.

It was difficult pretending to be serene in front of her friends. They knew her too well. She went to a party the second week he was away and got drunk on white wine, and was very manic. Even drunk, none of the men there appealed to her. She liked them all, jabbered to all of them, kissed one whose name she did not bother to find out, but she did not want to go to bed with any of them, and she went home alone. She woke up with a hangover, a wasted day, and lay in bed remembering the old days, the wasted old days in bed with hangovers, or men she didn't care about, and good resolutions she knew she would not keep.

Matthew called every day. She finally said tentatively

that she loved him, but it was more of a question. He answered that he loved her too. She did not ask him when he was coming back.

She had lunch with Bernice. Bernice had two drinks and then poked the food around on her plate with one tine of her fork.

"I might as well tell you," Bernice said. "I'm separated."

"You?"

"Yes. Hank's living in New York and I've got the house and the kids. It's a trial separation. It was my idea."

"I'm surprised," Carol said. "You of all people really wanted to get married, and you really wanted to marry *him*."

Bernice sighed. "Oh, didn't I? How I used to lie on the couch and cry because I thought he would never call me again. My parents thought I was having a nervous breakdown. How I dreamed of marrying Hank, and the intrigues, the planning. I didn't know what marriage was. I just thought it would be perfect. And do you know what?"

"What?"

"Hank is dull."

Carol didn't know what to say.

"Hank was always dull," Bernice went on. "I mean, we had no interests in common. He likes football and business. I like people. Before we were married he never talked to me about anything that interested me, but I was so in love with him I used to pretend I was fascinated by all those dull things he liked. I kept thinking that once we were married it would all be different. We would be *married,* so we would have that in common. We could talk about our marriage."

"And didn't you?"

"Talking about marriage is dull," Bernice said. "Pretty soon we didn't talk at all. We talked about the kids—you know: How are the kids? What did they do today? Why aren't they home yet? Then we moved to the country, and that was even worse. I was so bored I felt as if I'd disappeared. The only thing that saved me was I had a few love affairs."

"I always thought you were so happy," Carol said stupidly.

"Oh God. Happy? The only time I was happy was when I was in love with a man I went with for two years. I loved him and he loved me. We could talk about everything. I was so happy everybody noticed, except Hank. He never noticed anything. I thought then of leaving him and marrying this man; he really wanted me to. But there were too many problems."

"Was he married too?"

"Well, that. And my children and his children. But the main thing was he was an artist and he didn't have any money."

"And now?"

"Oh, I don't see him anymore. That was a long time ago. But it was a beautiful thing and I'll always remember it. It helped me survive. That and one or two other love affairs I had. They were the only beautiful things in my life."

"Did Hank fool around too?" Carol asked.

Bernice shrugged. "Oh, sure, a few times. But it was nothing. He always told me. It was just because some girl made up to him and he was flattered. It was just his male ego."

"Do you think you'll get divorced?" Carol asked.

"I don't know," Bernice said. "I have a lot of friends, I know men, I could get along. We'll see."

Wouldn't it be funny, Carol thought, if Matthew's wife knew about her and thought it was just his little ego trip, while all the time she was going with someone and thought it was the most beautiful thing in her life —and Matthew didn't have the slightest idea. No matter how much a stranger Matthew's wife was to her, she was sure his wife was nearly as much a stranger to him. The minute married people disappointed each other in any way, they seemed to start to hold themselves apart deliberately, as a punishment. The housewife gives a party and bakes fortune cookies; in each one she puts a piece of paper that says, "Help! I am a stranger in a marriage." She gives one to each person there except her husband.

38

The third week seemed very long. Carol thought about men she had known years ago. She remembered the ones who felt threatened because they knew she could walk out, and that had made them hostile.

Matthew . . . she thought.

She had become vulnerable through loving him, so why could he not have become vulnerable through loving her?

39

Carol had dinner with her parents. They no longer asked her so many questions, and she had learned not to let them upset her. They tried to make conversation on general subjects. She knew her parents were both extremely intelligent people, and she had seen them do a Jekyll and Hyde act many times in front of her friends: instead of discussing diets, illnesses, and the mercury count in tuna fish, they turned erudite and amusing. What was it about families that made them so boring with each other?

She had champagne and they had Cokes. Her father said if she would go to Israel with them they would pay for her trip. Her mother said she wished Carol would take them to London and show them around. Carol said maybe some day they would do all those things. Now they had become the children and she had become the grownup. They wanted her to show them the world. They seemed afraid to find it by themselves.

Her mother was scrutinizing Carol's face. "Your eyes are so small," she said. "Why are your eyes so small? They used to be so big when you were a little girl."

"My head was smaller."

"No, you've done something to them."

"Eye makeup has changed. I used to wear a lot."

"No," she said. "Your eyes have gotten small."

That night when Carol got home she looked closely at her eyes in the mirror, and then she put on eye liner for the first time in nearly two years. She wondered if Matthew thought her eyes were small. He had always told her she was beautiful.

She took off all her makeup to go to bed and wondered if all mothers were crazy by nature, or only hers. Who else but a mother or a four-year-old would make a comment like that?

Her next-door neighbor said the building was having an ecology meeting, and they had decided to use Carol's apartment because she was the only one who hadn't shown up to sweep the street and she had to do something. She agreed if he would bring the chairs. So about thirty people showed up, jammed into Carol's living room and front hall. Women were running around feeling her lampshades and asking her where she had bought her rug. They were calling their husbands to come look at this picture, that material.

The next-door neighbor read the petition he had written and everybody voted for it. An elderly couple asked Carol if she would trade apartments with them because theirs was too big now that their children had gotten married. Carol said no. She served no refreshments but nobody seemed to mind.

The next day Carol's landlord told her that six people had called him asking if they could have her apartment when and if she moved out. She looked carefully during the next few days but she couldn't tell if their street was any cleaner.

Matthew called and said he would be home the next day. He didn't say "back," he said "home."

40

Matthew called when he arrived and Carol went to the apartment. He looked different, thinner, worried. He held on to her. Then he gave her a box containing a gold bracelet. She had forgotten about the piece of string, but evidently he had not lost it.

He had a different car, not the limousine but one he had rented which he drove himself. They drove to the country for dinner because it was a beautiful day. On the road he seemed to relax. He looked happy. He took her hand.

"I love you," he said.

A few days later they were going over their liquor supply in the apartment and discovered they had no vodka. "How could we have no vodka?" he said.

"Did somebody drink it?"

"We have to keep track of these things. I never let myself get out of any kind of booze."

"We drank it that night we had our fight," she said.

"What fight?"

"Our big fight. When you said you didn't love me anymore."

"We don't fight."

"Yes we do," she said.

"I promise not to fight with you anymore."

"Yes you will."

"Yes I will," Matthew said. They both laughed.

41

Because she was reading so many books Carol began to discover the kind of books she was most drawn to. They were the stories of young women who went mad because people wanted them to conform. Sometimes it seemed to her that they were sane and the system was mad, which of course was the purpose of the story as the author told it. She identified with these heroines in every way except their giving up and going mad. You didn't have to run away inside your own head when you could just run away, or even stand there and fight back. Still, she could understand why those books were lionized by a small cult and generally not too well received by the people who make best sellers. Some people love to see other people have their nervous breakdowns for them. But most people get nervous at the whole idea that someone would hate the way *they* lived so much that it would destroy them. Maybe they identified too.

"My kids swim like fish," Matthew said. "I gave them lessons when they were three months old, before they were afraid, but then a few years later they had to learn all over again."

Carol remembered suddenly why she had been a terrified nonparticipant at athletics. "When I was four I had swimming lessons," she said. "I wasn't scared at all. But the instructor—he was a guy—he said he had to teach me the meaning of fear. So he picked me up by my ankles and held me under. I thought I was going to drown. He said to my parents, 'Now she knows the meaning of fear so she won't ever be afraid again.' I never put my head into the water after that."

"If anybody did that to my kids I would kill him," Matthew said.

"Then my parents tried ice-skating lessons. They wanted me to be good at something. They said I would have fun if I was good at some sport. The first time I never fell down, so the instructor—another guy—said he had to make me fall down so I wouldn't be afraid to. He kicked my feet out from under me. He did it three times. After that I was always scared to death and I hated to skate. Why do people always want to show you The Meaning of Fear?"

"If anybody did that to you I would kill him," Matthew said.

"I don't know why people always want to teach you The Meaning of Fear when you find out soon enough by yourself," she said. "I don't really blame them, though. I suppose it was just the educational system in those days."

She didn't know why she hadn't answered what he had just said and said thank you. She was too busy listening to what he had said going into her mind.

42

She began to wonder about Matthew's wife. If a man has been more or less living with another woman for two years, wouldn't his wife notice any changes in him, or wouldn't she change herself? Carol could hardly imagine that some well-meaning friend (substitute evil, gloating friend, for that's what all well-meaning carriers of gossip were) had not already told her that Matthew had "someone." Perhaps his friends were all saints, or perhaps they didn't care, or perhaps they were afraid of Matthew's wrath. He was not a pleasant person when he was angry. Perhaps his wife had known about the "someone" for a long time, and was just waiting. That would be clever. Or perhaps she did not really care. Carol had seen those women, in love with their marriage instead of the man they were married to, relieved not to have to share his bed and dreary company, comfortable in their place in the world as a Wife, without having to act like one. They got married because the world had expected it of them, and so they expected it of themselves, and then they stayed married for the same reason. Perhaps they were once in love, perhaps they thought love would come afterward, the way her analyst had.

So, rather tentatively, Carol became a spy. If the phone rang (Matthew always answered it at night), she pretended not to be listening, but she turned down the records or the television on the pretext of not having the sound annoy him. She listened. She left the room so he could be himself, and then she hovered out of sight to hear. His wife didn't call often, but Carol learned to tell from his voice that it was she. He had a special tone for her: polite, friendly, a bit exasperated. It was less exasperated than the tone Carol took with her parents, because his wife did not affect him as much. He often slammed the phone down afterward. Carol didn't know if she called him at the office too. She didn't ask. She didn't ask if he called her from the office, although once in a while he called from the apartment at night to talk to his children. His children did not call him. Perhaps they had been told that long distance was too expensive for children. Children are lazy anyway.

It was difficult to know what his conversations with his wife were like because she did all the talking. He gave an occasional grunt, and said, All right, I'll take care of it. Carol supposed she was telling him that the washing machine broke, there was a present to be sent, that she needed a new car, that a bill had been mailed to the wrong place. What else could he take care of, her heart?

Although Matthew's wife evidently depended on him to take care of the things Husbands took care of, she did not seem clinging. She could not be a clinging woman and survive this long without him, not only the time he had known Carol but evidently for many years before that. Carol remembered the pantry of their house in California: the cases of Spaghetti-O's, the boxes of Cocoa Pops and Captain Crunch and Pop Tarts, the jars of peanut butter with grape jelly swirls and Mister Marshmallow, the Campbell's tomato soup cans lined up like a little army, the gallons of ice cream in the freezer, the Good Humors, the Ice Stix, the hamburger patties and veal patties and chicken patties neatly wrapped in freezer paper and labeled, the frozen chili extra-mild, the packages of frozen corn. All the things children like and grownups hate and avoid. And what for the grownups? Hors d'oeuvres, party food, tiny patty shells, tins of pâté, celluloid cylinders of empty snail shells, small glass jars of black caviar, cans of hearts of palm slightly rusted along the edges because they had come all the way from Brazil. What did *she* eat?

That pantry was a life, a person. Carol saw a million women in it, the surburban wives of America alone in a world of children and calories.

One day she asked him, "Would your wife ever leave you?"

"Never," he said. "She likes being married."

Her question was not a hint or a wish, it was just an

assessment of the other woman's independence. Carol had liked thinking of her as a fiery woman who would throw him out if she discovered he did not love her anymore, but his wife had even cheated herself of that. Perhaps staying took more strength. Every suburban house has a wife in it, bland, permanent, immutable, as much and as little a part of the life within as the well-tended lawn outside. You might as well rip up the lawn and replace it with a skating rink as try to rip out the wife inside. What would people think? She left him? (She tore up the lawn?)

There was an accident on the subway; three cars were derailed. An angry politician appeared on television. "A breadwinner leaves his home in the morning," he said, "and his wife doesn't even know if he can come home safely at night." A breadwinner? Why didn't he say, A man who is loved leaves his home in the morning?

How would I know? Carol thought. I have never been at the mercy of a breadwinner.

One night when Carol and Matthew were in a New York restaurant eating their high-protein, dry broiled, dietetic dinner, she asked him, "What is your wife like?"

He thought for a moment, looking puzzled. Then he said slowly, "She's a good mother. She's a *very* good mother."

Ding dong, the witch is dead. Carol never really thought about her again, because it made her feel sad.

43

Bernice got divorced. For a while she went through a phase of guilt toward the children and wanted to stay home and spend time with them. The children didn't want to spend time with her. They wanted to be with their friends and have fun. Her social life with people of her own age was not what she had expected it would be. Her married friends were afraid she wanted to have fun.

Carol and Matthew took Bernice to dinner. "When you get divorced," she said, "you find out who your real friends are."

She was all dressed up in chiffon, with a ring on every finger, as if she hadn't been out in a long time. She had never met Matthew before, although she knew about him from Carol, and she directed all her conversation to him. It was as though she wanted to make it absolutely clear that she was no longer one of those country club wives who sat in a group and directed their sole attention to the other wives.

"It was a very friendly divorce," Bernice said to Matthew. "We're still great friends. But we were married for twenty years and I was very young when we got married. The two people who got married twenty years ago weren't the people we are now. I felt as if I were drowning. We didn't have anything in common. I'm glad we have the children, and now they're old enough to be people, not children, so they can be my friends. I enjoy them. I want to find a life for myself. I want to find a job."

"What can you do?" Matthew said.

"I want to work for one person. I want to help him. I could be very good at that."

"What kind of person?"

"I don't know. A producer. A star. I could be very good as a troubleshooter." She toyed with her rings. They were all expensive looking. "I know the difference between being lonely and being alone. I like being alone and I'm never lonely. I first started thinking about breaking up when I read Kate Millet's book. Women's Lib changed my life. This wasn't an overnight decision. I thought about it for a year. Then I told him I had to be alone to find myself. He understood. I'm not in love with him, but I *love* him, I really do. I just can't stand being married to him, being a wife, running a home—it's not enough. I said to myself, I'm still young, there's still time. The only hard part was telling my mother. She cried when I told her. She said, 'All my life my dream has been to have grandchildren.' I said, 'But you do have grandchildren.' She kept crying. I held off telling her as long as I could because I knew she would be upset. It was terrible."

When they left the restaurant Bernice got into her

Mercedes and drove back to the suburbs. She was alone and Carol felt lonely for her.

"Women are crazy," Matthew said. "You're all crazy. You're born crazy."

"Why?"

"Because she was married for twenty years and she wasn't afraid to tell her husband she wanted a divorce; all she was afraid of was telling her mother." He laughed.

44

On a hot summer morning in the second year of Carol and Matthew's life together, Matthew's father had a heart attack on the subway going to work and died. It did not seem ironic to Carol that a man whose son had a limousine and chauffeur should be going to work on the subway; she understood that kind of pride. What seemed ironic was that it should have been in the newspapers. Why should someone who is loved so much by the people who know him have to become known to strangers because he happens to die in a bizarre way?

It was a shock because no one had known he had a

bad heart, but perhaps he hadn't; he was old, and old people die of everything and the doctor calls it something. Matthew took it well because his father was an old man, he'd had a happy life despite the hardships, and most of all because they had made peace with each other while he was alive. The viewing would last several days, then there would be the funeral; there were things to be done, affairs to be settled, and because he was the only son he was busy. The best thing about Matthew, Carol thought, was that he never got hysterical. The men in her family were hysterics, as were the women; they seemed to enjoy it.

The cable from Matthew's wife in Paris said: ARRIVING TOMORROW 9:00 A.M. SEND CAR. LOVE.

"Shit," Matthew said.

Carol packed everything she owned: her clothes, her makeup, the little bottles of pills with her name on them, her toothbrush, magazines she had brought with her name and address on the subscription label on the cover; then there was not enough room for them in her suitcase, so she tore off the subscription labels so she could leave the magazines on the coffee table. She was as precise and careful as if she had just committed a crime. There was still too much for the suitcase, so she packed shopping bags. Matthew watched all this with a kind of fear.

As for herself, she felt nothing. Zero. Calm, efficient searching for anything that would make her visible, methodical search and destroy. But she had a stomach attack and she knew what she was really feeling: that their life together was beautiful as long as it was contained in their fantasy, but there were things that could happen to make it not exist. She was, after all, his girl, not his wife. Sanity demanded she disappear. And she was thinking: *She will be sleeping in my bed. She will never know it is my bed, or that I will have a long time afterward feeling I would like to throw it out and buy another because she, not I, wrecked a marriage, mine, and she, not I, was the intruder. But no matter how much he loves me, I am the outsider, and if he should die before me I would have to disappear again and then it would be exactly as if I had died too.*

Carol's calm face did not deceive Matthew. He was in pain for her, and she thought he was a little afraid that once she had gone she would never come back.

"You don't have to do that," he said. "This is a small apartment, maybe she'd rather stay at a hotel."

"Nonsense," Carol said.

"You don't have to take it with you," he said. "Just leave the suitcase in the closet, no one will notice."

"I need my stuff."

"She won't be here that long."

"Packing for a week is the same as packing for a month," she said, having read it somewhere in one of her women's magazines: Tips for Travelers. (What it had actually said was packing for a month is the same as packing for a week because there are always cleaners, but it seemed a suitable quote for the occasion anyway.)

When Matthew came back from the funeral parlor he took Carol and her things home to her apartment in his limousine, the same one that was to transfer his other wife the next morning. Carol wondered what the doormen would think at "the" apartment, and decided that if any of them dared to mention his wife to her, she would say she was his mother. Then he took Carol to a very nice restaurant for dinner, they had a bottle of wine that was much too expensive, and they drank it and looked sad and tried to be cheerful. Carol thought he was also angry. She knew she was, particularly because she had no right to be. When she was high she considered calling up an old lover the next day, or perhaps some guy who had wanted her and had never been her lover. Then she decided there was no reason to be destructive. Her destructive days were over; Matthew had taught her that.

Matthew stayed over at Carol's apartment and it was as if they were dating again. But he had never slept at her apartment before. He had already decided to send the driver to get his wife without accompanying him, but he got up at six o'clock anyway because he was nervous.

"I hope she likes the apartment," Carol said.

"I'll call you. Will you be in?"

"I'll be in and out."

"Then I'll keep calling till I get you."

When he left she wondered what to do with herself. She didn't want to call any of her friends to take her to dinner because she was afraid they would enjoy the drama of the situation too much, and she just wanted to forget about it. The only thing that made it all seem real and not like some nightmare she had invented was that he had told her three times that he would sleep on the couch. Once would have been enough; she knew he would sleep on the couch. But she couldn't help wishing that his wife would be the one to sleep on the couch. And then Carol felt sorry for her. Perhaps she had known about them all along and had been waiting all this time for an appropriate situation to arise so she could come to see for herself. It must take either extreme courage or extreme cowardice to do that. Carol didn't think she could ever be so patient.

She went to the grocery because there was nothing to eat in the house and the milk had gone sour.

At the supermarket she saw her married neighbor. She had her little boy in the shopping cart and he was screaming.

"I never see you at the store," her neighbor said. "I thought you never ate."

"I eat out," Carol said.

"What a shame, that gorgeous kitchen. I hate mine. I have my eye on your apartment. We'd like to rent it and tear through the wall. Then I can have a kitchen for the kids and one for us."

"The landlord won't let you," Carol said.

"He will. I asked him. Why don't you get married and move out?"

"Because I plan to marry a poverty-stricken painter and we'll live in my apartment. Forever. We'll never have children."

Her face fell. Carol left her standing there, the child still screaming, and she hoped he screamed all the time until he went to college.

God, why did everybody want to get rid of everybody else? There must be a place she could live with Matthew, a farm or an island, where people weren't always shoving each other for room.

When she had put away her groceries, she wondered what to do with herself.

"To what do we owe this honor?" her mother said.

Carol was tempted to tell her.

How wonderful it would be to have a mother she could confide everything to, who would never criticize her, never be shocked, never cry at night because she was coming to a bad, lonely end. But it was asking too much to ask your mother to accept you, not because she was another generation but because she was your mother. Carol wondered if Matthew's mother would have been as tolerant of his life if he had been her daughter instead of her son.

Thinking about Matthew's mother, she realized she wouldn't have her own parents around forever. She knew it meant eating one of her mother's tasteless, burned casseroles, but she didn't care; she wanted to kiss her father, look at his thin, white hair and thin, lined face and be glad she had him. He was a strong old man: he had lived through forty-five years of those wretched casseroles, but she missed him already.

She brought a bottle of vodka to their apartment because she knew they had only weird things to drink which people had brought when they were invited to dinner.

She had also brought several books she thought they would enjoy, and her mother put them on the shelf as if they were precious because her daughter had given

them to her. Carol wondered if she would bother to
read them. Her mother didn't read much. In fact, Carol
didn't really know what she did all day, although she
said she was always busy. Carol thought she cleaned the
house before the maid came. She told her that once and
her mother got angry, and then she told her it was an
old joke and she hadn't meant it. Then her mother said,
"You always have to watch them, they never get it
right."

Her father made drinks and Carol got drunk, although she tried not to show it.

"Ooh, another?" her mother said.

"Where else can a daughter get drunk if not in the
safety of her parents' home?" Carol said.

"Just as long as you don't get drunk when you're out
with boys. Does someone always take you home?"

"They're not boys anymore," she said.

"Well, men. Whatever you go out with. I hope you
have lots of dates and know a lot of nice people."

"I do."

"That's good. A mother worries."

"Don't worry."

"I want you to be busy and have a nice time."

Carol thought it was her way of saying that she had
resigned herself to the idea that she intended to remain
single, but she didn't want her to be an old maid, and
she was pleased. But then her mother said, "Maybe
you'll meet someone nice and want to get married."

"Marriage isn't always that great."

"How do you know unless you've tried it? We're
happy."

"Maybe I will," Carol said, to shut her up.

"Anyone on the horizon?"

"You haven't asked me that in years."

"Well, I'm entitled to ask you that once every ten years, aren't I?" she said, smiling.

"Okay, you can ask me again in ten years."

"Please God," she said.

When Carol got back to her apartment, after accepting the cab fare her father pressed on her (they were always afraid she would take the bus and get murdered) and reassuring her mother four times that the doorman was always awake and always in the lobby, she felt rather cheerful because her mother had annoyed her just enough to get rid of the guilt she felt at not seeing them often enough. She called her service and they said Matthew had called. She put on the television set and made herself another drink. She missed Matthew terribly. At the supermarket she had bought a whole carton of cigarettes and she planned to smoke them all, tonight.

She went to sleep after the end of the 3 A.M. showing of *Way Down East*, but she did not sleep well; the room smelled of smoke (she had made it through two packs but not the carton) and the air-conditioner was making strange banging sounds as if it was going to quit. She got up early, to another relentless sunny day, and realized it was the day of the funeral. Funerals terrified her, and she was relieved that she was spared this wifely duty. A long, empty day stretched ahead of her, but she had a lot of work to do, and it was not so bad being single.

It was unfortunate that the book she had chosen to

read was about a girl's unhappy love affair, because her mind kept wandering away from this fictional life to her own. She could not help inventing drama and imagining what Matthew's wife would say to him and what he would say to her. Maybe she would tell him she was sick of him, or perhaps he would get angry and say he was sick of her. But they had a tragic event in common, so they would probably both try to be kind. She who hated to travel and leave the children had made a loving gesture to be by her husband's side; who could see evil in that? Carol could. Now that his wife was here, maybe she would decide to stay and reconcile with him, try to make their marriage what it once was a long time ago. But that sort of thing was only possible in those women's magazines: "Dear Doctor Lovelorn, my husband is an alcoholic who beats me and sleeps with young sailors, what should I do?" "Dear Mrs. Tsuris, stay with him, you are joined together forever in the eyes of God and a divorce would be bad for our readers."

Carol made a sandwich and started drinking Bloody Marys—after all, she had nobody to impress. She looked in the bathroom mirror to see if she looked much older than she had when Matthew had first met her; and it seemed as if she did. No more summer days in the sun for her, it made the skin look like a prune. She should do something with her hair, have it cut? She pulled the skin of her face but it was still too tight for a face lift. At least his wife was older than she was, and so was he. The fluorescent lights in bathrooms are the worst thing for the ego, so she had another drink and decided to forget it.

The truth is, she was rather enjoying the situation. She had never claimed to be unselfish. In his absence she was the center of attention. It gave her a mean little thrill.

He called that night from a bar and said his wife was booked on a plane the next day. Carol did not ask any questions. He seemed cheerful enough and said his mother was holding up well. The real shock would come later when there was nothing more to be done and she realized she was alone. Carol wondered to herself what good it was to have a long, happy marriage when the desolation afterward was so great. Better to be alone and miserable all your life and never care about anybody. Then you could never lose anything. Protect yourself.

She stopped drinking so she would be able to work, and worked until four in the morning. Then she broiled a steak, ate it, and went to bed.

The next day Matthew called and said. "Tell me when you want me to come get you."

"Now," she said.

She repacked the few things she had unpacked for her needs and was ready when he arrived.

"All went well, I take it," she said.

"Fine."

"What did she think about the apartment?"

"She said, 'I see you're getting along very well on your own.'"

"And what did you say?"

"Nothing," he said. "I was afraid of what I would answer."

She didn't know what more she had expected. It occurred to her that life for rich people who wanted a well-ordered life was a simple matter. The only really dramatic things that ever happened, the things you couldn't control, were sickness and death.

45

"I'm going to France to see my kids," Matthew said.

"When are you going?" Carol asked.

"The end of the week. I want to see how they're getting along. Besides, I haven't had a vacation for a long time and I'm tired."

"It will do you good. How long will you be away?"

"Two weeks, I think."

She watched him pack. "You won't miss me," he said. "You'll see all your friends and have a good time."

"I'll miss you anyway."

"You'd better."

"I can't understand wives packing for their husbands," she said. "I could never pack for anyone."

"Nobody's ever packed for me," he said. "I wouldn't let them. *I* pack."

"I want to go to Rome," she said.

"Why don't you wait till it's cooler and we'll go together?"

"Okay." She couldn't go anyway; she didn't have enough money and it was the wrong season of the year to get a magazine assignment at the last minute. All the editors were away on vacation. Everybody is tired in the summer; your brain fries.

Carol didn't go with him to the airport; she never did. She wondered if going to see his kids had something to do with his wife's visit, if she had threatened him as wives do with the fact that they were in their difficult adolescence without him, that his daughter might begin having sex too early, running off at twilight to sleep with a no-good French beach boy, or that his son might be sleeping with a beach boy, both his children looking for a father image, all his fault. Or probably he just missed them. It wasn't worth worrying about.

Carol managed to get herself invited for the weekend to the beach house of some people she didn't know very well, and she was the perfect guest, washing dishes, making sangria, chipping in for the food, sleeping a lot. It was fun. She sometimes liked to have many people around her, especially if she didn't have to talk to them all the time. The first invitation led to a second, from people she had met there. She got tan, despite her resolution not to sit in the sun and turn into a prune.

At the end of the two weeks Matthew came back. He rushed into the apartment, looking harried and nervous. His face was red from the Riviera sun, but his eyes were wide and he reminded Carol of a white rabbit. He put down his bags, changed his clothes, and made a drink.

"I decided something," he said. "If you want to."

"What?"

"I want to marry you."

46

"You don't have to change your life," Matthew said. "You can keep your apartment if you want to."

"Well, if I got married I'd want to do it all the way," Carol said. She was still trying to let the idea sink in. Her first momentary reaction was great joy and relief, but then she felt panicked. It wasn't as if she'd wake up married tomorrow; he would have to get divorced first, and that might take years. She had read a book on divorce and it sounded ugly and full of fights about money and children, all the love the two people had felt turned into as strong a hatred.

But people got divorced all the time and it wasn't her business. What was her business was if she could marry, and if being married would change everything, change her, and eventually ruin everything. She could not even imagine changing the name on her charge plates. Could she be Mrs. So-and-so, a no-name appendage? People would say what a good catch she'd gotten, and it would make her angry because they could never understand how much she loved him and what a good catch he really was to her because of that.

People would also be relieved. Her parents would be relieved to feel she would be taken care of after they were gone. Her friends would be triumphant—the dream of the poor little girl in the shadows, the patient little girl growing older and finally breaking up a marriage, had finally happened, even though there had been no marriage to break up. Carol could just see one of the bachelor girl magazines she had worked for calling up to gush would she please write the true story of how she had accomplished this feat. She would scream an obscenity at them and hang up. And other people, those predatory women at parties, would look at Matthew differently now because he was with his wife (substitute Small Brown Mouse) instead of that formidable enemy his Girlfriend.

"I have to think about it," she said. "This was really kind of a shock."

"Okay, you think about it," he said calmly, and poured her a glass of wine.

But she knew he was thinking about it. Nobody wants to be rejected. He had offered to make a sacrifice for her, because he loved her, because there was something conventional about Matthew under all the not caring what people thought, because he wanted her to be totally accepted and happy. But she was happy now. They didn't want children, they already had a home, a life. Even if he was divorced he would still have to go away to see his children, and his wife would probably not want her around. Carol knew it was possible to put such orders into a divorce settlement: you can't bring That Woman around to corrupt The Children.

If Carol married him, what marriage would mean to her was that they loved each other so much that they had finally made this public declaration to the world, because they had done everything else to prove it to each other. Without the wish to raise a family, for which they were both too old and had never had the inclination anyway, the only thing a marriage contract was was a public declaration of love.

And then, when you'd done everything, what would happen to the love?

She never wanted to tell him she was coming home and have him say, "Oh, shit." The strong could be as implacably indifferent as they were unreservedly loving. It was only the weak who carried on a pretense year after year when they really were bored to death with each other.

Married to Matthew. The joy and excitement rose up in her again: the square, the victim of forty years of propaganda, the little girl who would love to travel the world with her husband, being respected, being bowed and scraped to by hotel managers and bellboys. They did that anyway after a while, but it would be different because she would know, and so they would know.

Was she getting married to impress some greasy little hotel manager? Some hyprocritical maître d'? To be called Senora and Madame? After a certain age everybody called you Ma'am, it was a sign of respect. And soon people might be calling her Ms. It had been years since any stranger had called her Miss, or Honey, or Young Lady. They wouldn't dare.

Still, marriage to the only man she loved . . . You couldn't turn that down without a lot of thought. They didn't have to have a silly wedding, they could just do it quietly with a few close friends. They didn't even have to send out announcements if she was too lazy. Her life would not be diminished, she would not be a prisoner. Would he be a prisoner, having made the bond, having settled everything, and would he then feel cheated, bored?

"Don't look so scared," Matthew said. "We're married anyway. It's just that I'd like to marry you."

"Would it be different than now?"

"No. It would only be better, if that's possible. I know it hasn't been easy for you. I want it to be."

She supposed he thought her life with him was, if not tragic, at least bittersweet. Sometimes it was. She would have to think about it.

"If only I were twenty—" Carol said.

"But you are twenty. You'll always be twenty."

"Can I let you know?"

"Of course you can let me know. I'm not going to leave you. Where would you like to have dinner?"

47

Carol went to Princess Margaret Rose Tenenbaum's apartment for a drink. The princess could give her an entire half hour, then she had to take a bath and get ready for the hourly evening visit of her lover.

"Matthew proposed to me last week," Carol said, looking into her glass.

The princess hugged her. "When are you getting married?"

"I don't know if I want to."

She looked as if Carol had just told her she had donated her living body to medical science. "What do you mean you haven't decided? What is there to decide? You're dying to marry him, Carol. Why on earth shouldn't you marry him? There is no reason, tell me one good reason."

"I don't know."

"You'd be the only one of us who made it," she mused. "The dream really would come true for somebody."

"Give me another drink."

The princess poured more wine. "He could get divorced in Mexico," she said. "That doesn't take long.

You could plan on getting married on Valentine's Day. Wouldn't that be great? I always thought Valentine's Day was a romantic day to get married. Imagine . . . someone I know actually took a man away from his rotten wife."

"I'm not getting married for you, I'm getting married for me."

"Well, of course you are!"

"If I get married."

"There's no reason on earth, Carol, no reason on earth why you shouldn't marry that wonderful man."

48

Matthew and Carol had dinner in a restaurant with Ellen and Michael. When Carol and Ellen went to the ladies' room Carol told her. Ellen looked shocked.

"Do you want to *do* that?"

"I don't know."

"Why should you get married? You're just as good as married now. The only reason we got married is we were young and scared and conventional and we couldn't think of any other way to do it. I love being married, but . . . Well, you're different. You're braver than I am. You really made it work your way. I always admired you. If you got married, well . . . I mean, why should you be like everybody else? You're somebody special."

"I don't want to be special, I want to be me."

"But what you are is special. The way you live. The way you do what you want to, not what the world tells you to do."

"You've certainly changed. I remember when all you could think of was whether I was wasting my time with a married man."

"You made me change," Ellen said. "I saw through you that it could work."

49

"My God!" Bernice shrieked. "Don't get married! Marriage is a trap, it's death. Take it from me, I had twenty years of being buried alive. I'll never get married again. Don't you do it, it's not worth it."

50

"I think it's a very good idea that you marry him," Paul said thoughtfully. "Marriage is better."

"That's what he says," Sally said. "Don't get married. I wish I was single again."

"Doesn't it upset you to hear her talk that way?" Carol asked Paul.

He laughed. "She talks that way all the time. She'll never leave me."

"You bet I will. When I have all your money socked away in my own little private checking account."

"In that case it will take a hundred years because I'm poor."

"I can wait," she said.

"No matter what you say," Carol said, "you're the only couple I know who are really happy."

They both looked pleased. "That's what you think," Sally said. "I'm going to have my nose fixed and my teeth fixed and get silicone tits, and then I'm going to find myself a lover. Not someone too young—I think I'd like someone like Onassis."

"It would make your parents very happy," Paul said to Carol.

"What do they want with a son-in-law at their age?"
Sally said.

Carol realized it was hopeless to get advice from any
of her friends. They had used her to act out their own
fantasies, and none of them really cared what she felt.
It annoyed her so much to have become a symbol that
she felt like getting married just to spite them.

51

"I suppose you discussed it with all your silly friends,"
Matthew said.

"Naturally. You know me."

He shook his head. "Oh, Carol."

"Are you mad?"

"What can I do? I know you. You're supposed to do
what you want to do, not what those nitwits tell you to
do."

"I know that."

"What did they say?"

"Well, the married ones wanted me to stay single, and
the single ones wanted me to get married."

"They don't know anything about it. It would be different for us."

"I know that."

"And they don't care about you," he said, sounding sad and angry. "You know that, don't you?"

"Sure."

"Who do you love?"

"You."

"Wrong answer. Who do you love *first?*"

"Me?"

"Right. Remember that. You can't love me unless you first love you."

"Okay."

"And then who do you love?"

"You."

He nodded.

"Who do you love?" she said.

"Me."

"And then?"

"You." He shook his head. "No," he said. "I love me, but I love you more than I love myself."

How could she possibly not marry a man like that?

52

She remembered when she was young, not even eigh-
teen, her mother telling her stories about this boy or
that one who had proposed to a girl, and when she had
turned him down he went away and never saw her
again. It was supposed to be a warning, but it seemed
crazy to Carol: if he loved her enough to want to marry
her, why would he never want to see her again? She
supposed now it was a part of the craziness of those
times, that a romance either "came to something" or
you gave up. Or maybe those boys just wanted to get
married, if not to this one then to another one, anyone.

And then of course, later, there were the young men—
everyone had several—whom you slept with and got
along with and then if you got drunk or desperate one
night and said you'd like to get married, they would
disappear. Just mentioning marriage to them was such
a threat that it made them take the next plane to Puerto
Rico or Acapulco or change their phone number. They
were also products of the crazy times she grew up in,
when those young men thought that if a girl wanted to
marry them, she would manage it somehow because she

was a part of the system, that overwhelming army of "good" girls who would invade their frail fortresses, capture them, make them prisoners, husbands, bread-winners, bored slaves.

She also remembered Bernice wanting to marry Hank, crying every night waiting for him to call, who was his slave, who would do anything for him; and then later when he finally married her Carol remembered her lying in bed with morning sickness with their first child, and Hank running out to buy her a present.

"*Now* I've got him," Bernice had said viciously, and indeed she had, and part of it was because she was pay-ing him back for having made her suffer all those years, and part of it was because he had expected marriage would be like this and so he did not question the re-versal of emotional roles.

Carol remembered also a very beautiful girl, older than she, who had been going with a married man for years. In the beginning he had wanted to marry her and she had not wanted to marry him, and then eventually she wanted to marry him but it was too late; he did not want to marry her anymore. And finally he agreed to marry her, but before they could get married he died. She knew he had always loved that she was so beautiful, and she knew he would want her to look beautiful at the funeral, so she went to shop for a dress, holding herself together; and the salesgirl, seeing her in the lovely dress in the fitting room, had said cheerfully, "Oh, is this for your wedding?"

And Carol remembered the plain girl who lived with her mother and never dated, and finally when she was forty (which was very old to them in those days) she had met a much older man who loved her and they had gotten married. And six months later he died. But after that people no longer invited her to dinner or for weekends because they were sorry for her; they invited her because she was the distinguished rich widow. The worst part of it was that she had been a virgin when she married and she never went out with a man again. But those six months had changed her in her own eyes and her world's eyes from an unloved nobody to a real woman, and she changed, became almost no longer plain. She was satisfied: she had "lived."

Carol remembered the girl whose European parents offered a dowry to a fat, unattractive boy from out of town, but did not tell her. And then the day before the huge, elaborate wedding the boy sent her parents a telegram saying: REGRET HAVING TO CANCEL PLANS TERMS NOT GOOD ENOUGH. How the girl had cried! But then they found her someone else. She did not seem as excited as a prospective bride ought to seem, and thinking it was because she was nervous from her previous hurt, Carol asked her why she was marrying him in the first place. She looked vague. "I've wasted so much time on him," she said, "I might as well marry him."

Marriage . . . when Carol was a young girl in an office, the smug serene knowledge all young New York girls have that every married man can be had, that the casual invitation to lunch or a drink will end up in a proposition, not just from the old, drunk, ugly ones, but from the young, stiff, proper ones in their Brooks Brothers suits, all of them . . . the excuses: "My wife is in the country for the summer," "Marriage is boring," "My wife is in the hospital having a baby and we haven't slept together for two months." How they laughed at those married men, how superior they felt being twenty and knowing they were wanted for no better reason but that they were hard to get! And sometimes not so hard to get.

She remembered the men in the singles bars who took off their wedding rings, but the girls were smart; they could tell a married man with children by the fraying of his suit, the look of last year's shoes, by the very smell of him, so eager, so understanding, so shy, so anxious to please. "I have nothing to offer a girl like you." The bachelors thought they had everything to offer; you could get a cheap dinner and a turn on sheets that hadn't been changed since the last girl, and the chance to make coffee for them in the morning if they liked you, and maybe even the clap. How the girls laughed at them, and hated them, and resented them, and needed them, and some of those girls even married them.

And Carol remembered the "nice" boys who told her they went to call girls for their needs because it was easier, simpler, and they were saving themselves for a virgin. How could that lucky virgin compete with her image as the all-perfect mother figure? Eventually she would be sleeping with the married neighbor, whose own virgin as like as not would get around to sleeping with *her* almost interchangeable husband.

Carol remembered too much, she knew too much, and she was afraid of becoming "respectable" because that was so often a lie. She knew Matthew was different,

that there had never been a man exactly like him, nor a
woman exactly like her, but part of what made them
different and individual was that they had made no
promises or bonds with one another except their love
and need and respect.

Maybe she wasn't really so special, maybe she wasn't
important, but what she was was important to herself,
what she had made of her life was special, romantic.

She wanted him to come home to her every evening
because he was eager to, not because he had to for fear
she would scream and threaten. When you are not married you don't have to threaten to leave; the threat is
always there. Maybe they could make a good marriage,
maybe they would be different, good in the old way of
couples who stayed together for fifty years because they
loved only each other.

But she knew too much. The worst thing she knew
was what had happened to Matthew's marriage. Perhaps
that marriage would make him try harder, be surer of
his feelings now that he was a grown man. Being grown
had nothing to do with age. But looking at that marriage made her remember another story: a young man
was courting a lovely young girl and then one night he
met her parents. He looked at her ugly, bitter, mean
mother, and he suddenly realized what that girl he
loved was going to look like when she was old. So he
left her. And everyone he told agreed with him: they
didn't tell him that if he gave his girl a happier life than
her mother had, she would look different, they simply
agreed that if you could see the future beforehand it
was well to run away. Carol was not that long-ago girl

Matthew had married, she was herself. Still, she had seen him be indifferent, and it was something to think about.

She didn't know what to do. He didn't ask her anymore, he was letting her figure it out in her own time, but she could see that he was nervous, that for no reason at all and unjustly he felt as if he were being put on trial, and he was trying, and this broke her heart.

53

Carol had a dream. In this dream she and Matthew were married and they were traveling, staying at a hotel somewhere. He had gone out to a business meeting and she, assuming he would always be with her and take care of her like a Siamese twin, had somehow left her key in the room. Downstairs there was a beach and a bar. She had met several women her age and they were friendly, meeting, talking, drinking together. At one point in the afternoon she wanted to go upstairs to the room.

The desk clerk was an aging crotchety faggot, like those desk clerks in movie comedies of the forties. "I am

Mrs. Fitzgerald," Carol told him, "and my husband has the key. Would you have me let into our room?"

He looked at her with all the hostility of an aging employee with no money but much authority, of a homosexual looking at a young woman, of a male citizen looking at a wife. "Where's your key?"

"I left it in the room."

"If you're so stupid, you'll just have to wait for your husband. I can't let you into the room. Your husband should take better care of you."

"Do you think I'm a burglar?" It occurred to her in a burst of helpless rage that if she had said, "I'm Carol Prince," he would have reached into the box and whipped out her key with a nod of respect. But she was nobody, a wife, Mrs. Fitzgerald. Carol Prince the world traveling interviewer did not exist in this hotel, and it was too late.

"You just have to wait for your husband," he said, as if he meant zoo keeper.

She waited in the bar in the lobby with one of the nice women she had met, and they had several drinks. Carol thought of her key left stupidly in the room in trust that she would always be taken care of, and remembered wives who didn't even bother to take cab fare when they went out with their husbands. Did she have any money? She knew where Matthew was at his meeting, but some pride in her made her unable to phone him to complain.

"If you're going to be so nasty," she said to the desk clerk, "I won't pay for these drinks."

"Then I'll call the police," he said, rising.

"I'll charge them," she said.

"You can't charge them," he said. "Your husband has to pay for them. You'll just sit here and wait. Sit in the lobby."

"Then I'll pay for them," she said, and looked in her purse, terrified there was no money, relieved to find a few crumpled bills. She paid the waiter.

She wanted to scream obscenities at the desk clerk in a loud, hard voice, the way Matthew would do, threaten to take her business elsewhere, tell him he was nothing. She could even imitate the voice, the rage, the authority. But something prevented her—fear of not being believed, of being thrown out by superior masculine force because she was only a woman. She sat there crying without tears, in stupid, frustrated asthmatic rage, choking from the unfairness of it, the lack of dignity. She didn't care that people were looking, she couldn't stop the soundless, enraged crying. She knew Matthew would come back to save her and tell the clerk to go to hell, she knew she could call him now, but all she could do was cry and hate that desk clerk and the person she had become: a child again in the grip of mindless authority, trapped in her identity as Wife/Child, a person who belonged to someone who was respected but had no respect due to her as an individual because she was only a Wife/Child/Woman/Inferior/Stupid.

She should have taken her own room and said she was Carol Prince the journalist. Then he would have respected her.

54

"If you get divorced," Carol said to Matthew, "your wife will take all your money and you'll be broke."

"I know what I can do about that," he said. "I'll make more."

He looked young and strong and ready to take on the whole world.

"Your kids will hate me."

"They'll love you."

"It will be too much trouble."

"Why don't you let me worry about that?"

"I don't like to make trouble," she said.

"You can be free. You'll have your life. You can go off alone with your friends whenever you want to. If you find someone you love more than me, you're free."

"I don't want anyone else," she said. "I just want you."

He looked at her sadly. "You never want to marry anyone, ever."

"Maybe I'll change my mind."

"No," he said, "you never want to get married."

"Some people should never be married."

"That's true," he said. "I should never have been married."

"But you are."

"Yes," he said.

"You'll never leave me, will you?"

"No. Not unless you leave me. If you do leave me, I'll always be your friend and help you any way I can."

"But I'll never leave you," she said.

"Then it's all right, isn't it?"

"Yes," she said. "It's all right."

"It's all right."

"You're not mad at me?" she said.

"Why should I be mad at you?"

"I don't know."

"Then don't make up reasons."

"Okay."

It's all right. It's all right the way it is. It had to be, because for her at least, there wasn't any other way.

She wished she had met him when she was twenty. But then she wouldn't have been her and he wouldn't have fallen in love with her. And whoever she was when she was twenty she didn't love herself, nothing had happened to her yet, and if she hadn't changed she certainly wouldn't love herself today. It was funny: if she had been able to look into the future when she was twenty and see what she was today, she would have thought it was a tragic, dramatic end. But she was happy, and she felt she was lucky.

"I think there's ninety percent of you I don't understand," Matthew said.

"You're supposed to understand all of me."

"Do you want me to try?"

He sounded different, something strained in his tone, as if all the things he was going to understand might not turn out to be so endearing anymore. With love and goodness he had come offering the final charity, and the "indigent" had refused him, not through pride but through lack of need.

Do you want me to try? Strained. Menacing. She didn't answer.

*　　*　　*